From When She Turned Scary...

GW00778201

Young Bloody Mary

Keren Dibbens-Wyatt

MOGZILLA

Paperback edition: ISBN: 9781914426049
Text Copyright: Keren Dibbens-Wyatt
Cover by thebooktypsetters.com
Cover illustration: Rebecca Davy
Designers: thebooktypsetters.com
Printed in the UK by Imprint Academic Limited
First published by Mogzilla in 2023

Author's Acknowledgements:

I am grateful to Dr Sarah Morris for her informative website and YouTube channel, *The Tudor Travel Guide* and for kindly sending me a copy of Mary's itinerary. I am also indebted to the Tudor Times website, to Anna Whitelock for her book *Mary Tudor* and to Melita Thomas for her book *The King's Pearl*.

Many thanks to Paul Nolan of Mogzilla Books for the chance to write this book and for his support. Also, to Alison and Matthew for their confidence that I could.

Lastly, but not least, I express my gratitude to my husband and history enthusiast, Rowan, for his help and expertise as well as his loving encouragement and the endless cups of tea it takes to fuel an author.

Publisher's Acknowledgements:

Many thanks to Frances, Scarlet and Elspeth.

To Thea
Best Wishes,
KerenDW

MOGZILLA

www.mogzillabooks.ecwid.com

For Georgie, Elijah, Felicity and Jacob.

The Royal Family:

Mary Tudor: de facto Princess of Wales. Future Mary I and 'Bloody Mary'

King Henry VIII: Mary's father

Queen Katharine: Mary's mother

Henry Fitzroy: Duke of Richmond (referred to as 'Richmond') and Somerset, Henry's VIII's illegitimate son, Mary's half-brother and rival for the throne

Members of the Royal Court:

Lord Ferrers: a steward

Lord John Dudley: Chamberlain of the Princess's household

Dr Richard Fetherstone: Mary's Latin instructor

Giles Duwes: Mary's French teacher

Cardinal Wolsey: King's closest advisor and Mary's godfather

Margaret Pole: Countess of Salisbury and Mary's Lady Governess

Constance Pole: Countess Salisbury's daughter-in-law

Elizabeth (Lizzie) Pole: Constance's daughter

Lady Catherine Craddock (nee Gordon): chief Lady in Waiting and head of Mary's Privy Chamber

Mary's female attendants

Other Principal Characters:

Richard Shakespeare: tenant farmer, player and a certain playwright's grandfather

Abigail Shakespeare: Richard's wife and playwright

Marion de la Bruyere: The 'White Lady', a ghost

Prior William More: Prior of Worcester

Fictional Characters:

Lord Percival Puce: local lord

Lord Gravenor: another local lord

Matthew: stable hand

Hazel Lovelace: paid playmate of the Princess and her doppelganger (double)

Anne Knyvett: Lady in Waiting

Cecily Dabridgecourt: Lady in Waiting

Author's Note

This book is first and foremost a work of fiction. Although I've tried to place Mary and her real retinue in the right places at the right times, it is impossible to know for sure where she was for much of these childhood years.

Although many events are real, this story, and some of the characters, are fictional. Whilst we know people's names, we know precious little about them, so please use your imagination when reading the book. If you can do that, I'm sure you'll enjoy discovering more of the young Tudor princess and her path to becoming Bloody Mary...

1525

21st July

You never hear anything good about yourself if you eavesdrop, they say. Until today I've never understood that. I'm the darling of the realm, the King's Pearl, the sweet princess, and no-one would dare say anything against me. Why would they? But on this hot summer's day, stood behind the largest tapestry in the corridor by the throne room, my blood ran cold.

"She is no good to the Emperor now," I heard my father say. "Now he has France so firmly in hand." He sighed. "We will have to make other arrangements."

"Arrangements, Henry, what do you mean? A new betrothal? To whom?"

Mama sounded angry, but not as angry as I felt.

"Yes, a new marriage. But also," he paused, "something else."

I was on tenterhooks, as no doubt was Mama. I tried to keep very still and hoped the thunderous beating of my heart would not give me away.

"She may have to rule here as queen one day, the way everything is going," Father continued.

"Not here and France together?"

"Well, perhaps. That is something we can hope for, negotiate for. I will send Wolsey. But if Charles does look elsewhere for an empress, or Francois won't have her, Mary must learn how to rule."

This pleased me and softened my heartbeat. I did not want to be a mere consort. I strained my ears and stood on tiptoe.

"I am sending her to the Welsh Marches. I know she is bright. But can she govern? I will have her tested."

Mama gasped a little. My own heart sank at the idea of leaving but pumped harder again at the thought of a challenge.

"You are sending her away? We do not see her enough even now, when she lives across the river!"

"She is old enough. We are too soft on her. She must toughen up."

At this, he strode over to the side of the throne room, towards me. I was terrified. My father's rage is not something you want to see, let alone suffer.

"When shall she go?" asked the Queen quietly, resigned to both her fate and mine.

"Next month. It is all arranged."

"You did not think to consult me?" Mama asked, finding her voice.

Not wishing to hear my father's wrath, I slipped carefully from my hiding place, and thanked God that the kid leather soles of my shoes would not make a noise on the flagstones as I made my escape. My mind was tumbling over itself. I was to be sent to the Welsh borders! Was I going to have an adventure at last, having been coddled by the court for so long? And more importantly, could I handle it? What did I know about ruling?

Back in my room, I made my first decision. I took out the journal I had been given for my ninth birthday. I turned to the first blank page. I hurriedly wrote down all I had just heard. If I am going to have some adventures, then I want to remember them well.

25th July

When Mama came in to explain my fate, I managed to force sadness. Maybe listening at doorways isn't such a bad thing after all. It is good to be prepared. Mama, though, had been crying. She called me "*Mija*" and stroked my hair. I put my arms round her and asked why I had to go. Perhaps it could still be stopped, and I could stay near her and Papa. He was scary sometimes but a great deal of fun if you could keep him on your side.

I asked Mama lots of questions and she just smiled sadly, saying little. She does seem sadder lately. Father shouts more now and laughs less. I wonder if it's something to do with me. Is it because the Emperor no longer wishes to marry me? Did I do something wrong? Is that why they are sending me away? Mama says no and I should put such silly ideas out of my head, but ideas tend to stay put, don't they, once you've thought of them?

I wonder if I can take Guinevere with me. She is a fantastic hunter already, even though I've not been training her long, and a goshawk with sharp talons may prove useful in the Welsh Marches.

1st August

Thwack! The arrow hit the outer ring, just shy of the bull. I punched my fist in the air and held aloft the longbow which had been specially made for me.

The crowd cheered. I so enjoyed being the guest of honour at today's tourney. It was a great send off. I watched transfixed as soldiers, most with bows as tall as they were, and some missing fingers, hit targets hundreds of yards away. Mine was so short you couldn't call it a *long* bow. Father said a real one would take off my arm, and that he'd find me a husband more easily if I still had two.

"Marriage, is that true?" I said excitedly, which prompted a raucous belly laugh. "I'll never get to go to war though, will I?" I asked.

"Of course not. War is men's work. You might get to start or end them though!"

I wondered what he meant. I was about to ask him, but then he roared at me to fire up my next arrow.

"C'mon lass! People are waiting! Never disappoint your public!" he winked at me. "See if you can hit the bullseye this time!"

I held the curved wood of the bow, which even though it was made for me, was an inch taller than I was. I held my arrow against the string, and pulled back on it with all my might, trying to line the tip of the arrow up with the centre of the target. A serving boy stupidly ran across the target range, but it was too late, I'd already let go. The arrow ripped through the air, missing the fool's ear by a whisker.

"Bull!" roared the King, hoisting me upon his shoulders. "The King's Pearl hit the bull! She's a general in the making and no mistake!"

He roared again and I roared with him, raising my arms up in the air. In the distance I could see the serving boy getting a clip round the ear from his worried mother, who was carrying a tray of ale. Somewhere deep down I felt a rush of excitement and my cheeks flushed.

I am ashamed to admit it, and would only do so here in my diary, but I wondered what it would feel like to hit a person, and not just a target. Soldiers do that all the time, don't they, in battle? Injure someone. Take a life. Does that make you feel powerful? Like the grown-ups do after the kill on a hunt? Father says I will have to learn to hunt, when I get to preside over the Marches. I'm not sure if I'm looking forward to that.

2nd August

The day after my triumph, my father was ready for his own at the jousting competition. He always wins of course. Not just because no-one would dare beat him, but because no-one could! I wondered today if he was longing for a decent opponent for once.

It took three men to hoist him up, and Archibald, the seventeen-hand white stallion, strong as he was, still had to shift his hooves to take the weight. A squire handed up the lance and my father took it as though it were made of honeycomb. I'd tried to lift one once and couldn't even get the handle an inch off the ground. It was probably a good job that jousting was just for men. Mama says it's all about showing off and that is why Father enjoys it so much.

You couldn't look at him and not know he was king of all England. I gazed up at him on the horse. He did not look back. For one thing, the visor meant he couldn't move his head up and down, and for another, there was just one tiny slit in the metal for him to look through. He would need all his concentration to know just where to hit his opponent.

Today's first opponent was Sir Ellingham. He is tall and slim, and undoubtedly a skilled rider, but this would not help him. Father was both agile and strong – an unbeatable combination. I think I saw Sir Ellingham swallow in fear before his helmet was put on him, but it was hard to tell, sat where I was in the royal stand, at the centre of the long arena.

"God save the King!" I shouted, and the crowd took up the chant.

When Mother dropped the handkerchief, both horses sprang forward; Archibald blazing like a lightning bolt in the hot sun, Sir Ellingham's chestnut mare gleaming as she launched into a gallop. Even though they were so far apart, it seemed mere seconds before the thundering of hooves was right in front of us, clods of grass and earth flying up. The riders rode for each other, each with a pole poised in an outstretched hand. The crowd sucked in an anxious breath before shrieking with excitement as the King's weapon made contact first, knocking his opponent to the ground. The cheers which followed were deafening.

An hour later, Father returned for another ride – he clearly had some fire in his belly today. Later, at the feast, I found out why, and I shall tell of that shortly. Even to think of it now makes my face hot with anger.

It appeared that the visored knight about to challenge Father was not on the approved list, which explained the arm flapping and huffing and puffing of the beleaguered steward. I wondered who it could be. Father just saddled up and did not seem concerned, for he thought himself invincible. It was not until the two horses were pounding towards one another and both men let out great roars that I thought I recognized the man. If I was right, Father might not be so assured of victory.

The newcomer and the King both hit each other's shields, and scored the same points, until Father wobbled a little and nearly fell from his mount.

I had guessed right. Sir Charles Brandon, my father's best friend, pulled down his visor and grinned. There would be much drinking later, I was sure.

The King's team still won, naturally, and the feasting and quaffing of fine wines and ales began even before the sun went down. There was much talk and laughter, and reminiscing about the time their team broke the King of France's nose on the jousting field. I won't tell you the rude names they called him. At least, I won't write them down here, but I will remember them in case I need them.

I will tell the rest tomorrow, as I have written much, and my candle is at its end.

3rd August

I have had to wait until after luncheon to write the rest of what happened, but still I am determined to recall it all as well as possible. I was supposed to be the guest of honour at the feast, but all that seemed rather forgotten, with the unexpected arrival of Sir Charles and his stories. Most of them were not fit for a young princess's ears, prompting Mama to glare at Father and Lady Margaret to tut and shake her head. Father took no notice and just laughed louder and louder.

I noticed Henry Fitzroy sneak in and stand near the back of the hall. What was he doing there? He was a great favourite of Father's, being his son, but as one born out of wedlock it was beyond even my father's insensitivity to have him in the court with my mother present.

There was a man with him I'd never seen before. Tall,

richly clothed and pale. He had very blond hair and through it a streak of red. His grin lifted his red, wispy moustache, and I could see the glint of a gold tooth in the candlelight. Something strange was going on.

I had to wait for the speeches to find out what. King Henry, my father, stood up and raised his goblet.

"A toast!" he bellowed, and everyone shouted their approval. "To my daughter Mary, beloved princess and the King's Pearl, who shall henceforth rule at the King's pleasure at my seat in Ludlow as President of the Council of the Marches and on whom I confer the title Princess of Wales!"

A great roar of approval went up: "To the Princess of Wales!"

My face went red with all the attention and deepened when I stood and curtsied. There was lots of cheering and my mother smiled, clapped and looked very proud. Clearly, she hadn't noticed Fitzroy.

The King put down his drink and called for hush. One simple wave of his hand was enough to render the excitable throng silent. He beckoned, and Henry Fitzroy walked proudly forward. The tall stranger in dark clothes placed a hand on my half-brother's shoulder.

"And a second toast! To my son, the Lord Fitzroy, whom I send north, conferring on him the titles Duke of Richmond and Somerset, and President of the Council of the North!"

A muddled sound of confusion quickly gave way to cheering.

"To Richmond!" the cry went up. I sat down, feeling sick. I thought I might faint. I looked over at my mother. She too looked weak, but in her eyes there was both shock and anger which frightened me. She did not look at me. Instead, she blazed her fury at the King. What should have been my day, my moment of glory, had been tainted at its very end, and I felt as my mother looked.

As I write down what happened, I am no calmer, even though it is the next day. But my head is cooler. I can see it for what it is. I am in a competition – with the prize, the throne.

4th August

Guinevere looked at me today with the same deathly, impassive stare that Mama fixed on Father. I stared back at Guinevere, thinking I was glad not to be a vole or a shrew.

"Good little hunter, that one," gushed the falconer.

"Yes…"

I couldn't remember his name. Something to do with the countryside. Meadows? Fields?

"Hedges, Miss. You'll miss her, I'll be bound. Best goshawk we've got."

Hedges. Yes. He never did call anyone by the right title. I would correct him, but I couldn't be bothered. Besides, Father always said to just humour him, since he was irreplaceable. No-one could train a bird like Hedges.

"I will miss her," I replied. "Such a shame she can't come with me."

"She'd get disorientated, ma'am. She'd not know where she was and get lost." He shook his head.

"Can't have that."

"No, indeed."

I stroked the top of the hawk's head with my finger.

Risky with a bird you don't know, but Guinevere just relaxed a bit, as though the stroking made her sleepy. Her eyes half closed.

"And I will not be away too long, I don't think."

"They're sending you off to learn queening? Is that it?"

"Something like that," I smiled. "There is an art to being a princess, Hedges. Much like there is to training hunting birds."

"Aye, Miss," he agreed. "You have to learn how to show the prey that you are in charge. You have to rise above them and soar. Make sure they are afraid of you. Keep your talons sharp and your eyesight sharper."

"That's good advice," I said, rather astonished at its source.

"You don't spend your whole life round kings and queens without learning something, Miss. It's all just like nature. Life and death. Some has the power to take it, some has to suffer. Just how it be."

He fed a dead chick to a falcon whilst he spoke. I settled Guinevere back on her perch.

"I'll see you soon, dear one," I said. "Be good for Mister Hedges."

I turned my back on my feathered friend, and her trainer, and walked away, determined not to cry until I was in my chamber. Just like my goshawk, I must never show anyone my weakness. Not if I am to rule well.

17th August

I've not been able to write in my diary this fortnight. For one thing, I couldn't find it! Some fool of a servant packed it away. We set off from Ditton on Thursday last and stayed with my godfather Cardinal Wolsey for a few days. He wanted to give me some gifts and wait to hear that the plague had died down in Shropshire before we continued. He does take good care of me, and my father too. And the new green shoes he gave me are just lovely. A new rosary too, with a golden cross. All the ladies have been admiring it.

Since then, we've been stopping here, there and everywhere. I hate travelling. It would be bad enough just in the coach, but with this ridiculous entourage and cartloads of stuff, it is even slower going. I had much rather ride Sheba, but that would be unseemly on so long a journey. At least my stable hand, Matthew, is coming with us to look after Sheba. He is a few years older than me, and he loves her too. I trust him to take care of her. What's more, he has always been kind to me.

I hope Ludlow Castle will be warm and comfortable. The Prior at Worcester has sent a message to Lord John Dudley, my Lord Chamberlain, saying that we are welcome to stay with him until the building works at the Castle are finished, which doesn't bode well. I may be living out of trunks for some time yet.

Lady Catherine says to look upon it all as an adventure, and young Lizzie Pole piped up to say that we might all pretend we are pirates, or Robin Hood and his Merry Men. I gave her a glare. Foolish child.

"We are hardly at sea, Lizzie. Nor are we highwaymen. Do grow up."

I may only be nine, but too much imagination in a girl of nearly thirteen seems just silliness to me.

12th September

Today was a very special one, as we had a procession into Gloucester, my official reception to the ruling of the Marches. Sheba was draped in green velvet with blue trimmings, to match the new servants' livery that had been made for such an occasion. She looked splendid and knew it, not concerned that the gentlemen's horses were so much taller. I felt a bit like I was down a well, with Dudley on one side of me and the Mayor of the city on the other, as we paraded down the main street towards the gatehouse. But I was unmistakably right at the centre of things. No king or queen here to outrank me.

The streets were lined with commoners: merchants and farmers and their families, all cheering and stretching to get a glimpse of their princess. It was most gratifying. My heart felt warm, and all the travelling finally seemed worthwhile. Some of the little children threw flowers, and several went in front of the horses to strew rose petals for us to walk on. I had to pull Sheba's reins a few times to stop her trying to eat them. Eat the flowers that is, not the little children!

There was a fine acting troupe playing scenes from the Arthurian legends that I should have liked more time to stay and watch, and lots of entertainments, jugglers, fire-eaters and food stalls. A real party!

"God save Princess Mary!" a man shouted, and the rest of the people took up the cry.

I waved and smiled, feeling much admired and a little overcome. I don't always like being the centre of attention, but today it felt very good indeed. I patted Sheba's plaited mane and waved some more at all the cheering people. I do believe they really love me!

13th September

Even though it was only our first proper day here, Dudley insisted that we hold a first Council of the Marches.

"Your Highness, I know it's tiring, after all this travelling, but many of your subjects have heard of your coming and have been camped out for days, waiting to have you dispense your royal wisdom." He paused, and I knew there was more to it. "Quite frankly, Princess, the smell is beginning to get rather disturbing."

"You just want them all to go away as quickly as possible?" I ventured.

"Your Highness has a way of getting to the nub of the matter," he replied, ending his words with a bow.

He really wasn't joking about the smell. These folk, who had been waiting to have me pronounce upon their woes, had not dared leave their place in line to wash in the rivers. Lizzie Pole, with a huge, fresh nosegay tied to her waist and with pomanders hanging above her, almost fainted. She does like to make a drama out of everything, but in this case, I suspect not much acting was required.

The first few cases were easy enough: the disputed ownership of a cow, an uncertainty about an inheritance and something else too boring to even recall. It was nice to sit on a throne, even if it was only a chair on a dais, and feel I was actually ruling at last. Finally, I was learning how to be a queen.

I looked around the room as the next person came in. I was surprised there were now so many of the local lords here. They must have come to get a look at the princess they'd heard so much about. I felt a lot of eyes boring into me. My face flushed a little. There was one gaze more intent than all the others, from a tall pale man in a dark purple coat worn over matching hose. He looked familiar. I tried to ignore him and listen to the petitioner.

"If you please, Your Highness," the farmer mumbled into his beard, bent to the floor in a bow, "I don't have enough money to pay the Lord his taxes."

"Why is that?" I asked. "Have you not worked hard on the land?"

"I have, Your Highness." The man's voice sounded tired and wobbly, as though he might cry. "I've worked all the hours God sends, and not just in the daylight, neither. But the steward, he…." his voice faltered.

"Go on. What did the steward do?"

"He miscounted the sheaves from the harvest, and the fleeces from this year's ewes, and charged me more than I can pay."

"On purpose? Or was this a miscalculation?"

"The counting was so wrong, milady, I mean, Your Highness, I think it must have been…"

"I see." Lord Ferrers whispered a question to me, which I asked. "And is this steward prepared to let us see his reckoning, his accounts?"

"I… I don't know."

"I see." I conferred with Dudley. "Leave your name and the name of your farm with my steward, and I will have this looked into," I said, hoping I sounded wise and benevolent.

"Oh, I don't think that will be necessary." The tall man in his suave velvet stepped forward, his kerchief (which also matched) held over his nose. "I'll deal with this, Your Highness."

He bowed so slightly it was barely noticeable. I was not

impressed. The farmer was quivering near the floor. He looked frail and frightened.

"I will decide what is and is not needed, thank you. I do not appreciate interruptions at my court." Dudley grinned. I hoped he was proud of me.

"Oh, I do beg your pardon, Highness," the man continued. "I know this reprobate and will have the matter dealt with. One less thing for your investigators to worry about."

He moved the kerchief away for a moment, showing his red moustache, and bared his teeth in a smile. There was a glint of gold. Where had I seen him before? A memory stirred, and not a pleasant one.

"I do not have investigators," I replied, loudly and clearly, guessing this was a lie he wanted to spread about my court to the common people. "I have good, honest men looking out for other good, honest men. One of whom will come to see your steward. This is, presumably, a man in your employ?"

The man bowed a little again and narrowed his eyes.

"Dudley," I said, waving the upstart away, "Take this gentleman's name, for I do not believe we have been introduced. See that the truth outs, if you will."

"I shall, Your Highness. I believe this to be the Lord Gravenor. But I know little of these locals." The great gentleman (as he clearly believed himself to be) looked very angry.

"I am indeed," he said, through gritted teeth.

I believe I have made my first enemy here today.

16th September

I awoke suddenly in the night, in a sweat. I remembered where I had seen Lord Gravenor before! He was the sinister man standing behind my half-brother Richmond on the night of the tournament. But if he is a local lord here, why was he championing my rival for the throne who is headed north? Is he part of a plan I don't know about? Is he here to sabotage my court and make sure Henry looks a better prospect for the crown? I am all a-jitter now. So many questions. Who can I ask or confide in? I will tell Lady Margaret of course, but she is not a sly woman, more a kindly soul. Will she see what is going on? Can I really trust Dudley to help me either? Who do I really trust? I cannot go to Father or Mama. Father would want me to take care of myself and Mama would not believe me capable of dealing with such things and would worry rather than help.

Suddenly it came to me. Wolsey. I trust Cardinal Wolsey, my godfather. I will write to him tomorrow and ask his counsel. I can see this competition is only just getting started and it will be far less simple than two knights charging at one another on horseback. Some scheming may be required. I had better get good at that, and fast.

17th September

We went to a town market and festival this morning in the centre of Gloucester. I didn't really feel much like going, my stomach was all turned about after writing the letter to

Wolsey. But Lord Dudley had arranged the outing and he says I mustn't let my public down.

After the carriage to the town, I was taken in my sedan chair, since the weather couldn't quite make its mind up and Lady Margaret was concerned that I might catch cold on Sheba. On cobblestones it made me even more seasick than in the carriage. I would have preferred catching cold.

There were jugglers, only entertaining because the rain made them drop everything, and a tiresome jester, who I ignored. Many tables, too many to count, were laden with country wares: jams and pickles, chutneys and ales. My servants seemed to spend an inordinate amount of time sampling those. Then there were dairymaids, plying their wares, with different cheese wheels, curds and whey and pots of fresh cream. I had the pages take the chair closer and leaned out of my window, so I was under the awning of the stalls.

The women curtsied, though not low enough for my liking.

"Try some cheese, Your Highness?" asked one. Clearly, she did not know one only spoke to royalty once spoken to. Lord Dudley smiled at her and then at me. I most certainly didn't smile back.

"Such charming country manners, Your Highness."

"Dudley, I will try a bite of the Gloucester cheese," I said, in a bored voice. "Since everyone raves about it."

The woman looked proud and happy as she cut me a small slice. Mistress Pole took it from her. She took a tiny bite herself and we waited a few moments. Quite how the cheese might affect her quickly enough to protect me was a mystery, but it was protocol for an heiress to the throne. She nodded, curtsied and passed it on to me on a napkin.

I looked the woman right in the eye as I chewed a small mouthful of cheese carefully. Then, just as carefully, I spat it out on the ground.

"Revolting!" I pronounced, wiping my mouth with the napkin and pretending to gag. Everyone looked shocked, as I intended.

"The cheese, it does not please!" proclaimed the jester, who was hovering annoyingly nearby. "It's not royal approved – it's royal removed… for the chewing made for spewing!" he continued, and the crowd who had gathered around, began to laugh.

"Oh dear, I am so sorry," I said. "I simply could not eat THAT. Are you sure your milk is fresh?"

The woman, now as white as her produce, nodded.

"And your herd is quite well?"

Again, simply a nod. I waved the attendants to move me away from the stall and allowed myself a small grin. Now, as I write about it, I find myself a little ashamed. For it is not much of a victory for a princess of the realm to ruin the fortunes of a simple dairymaid. I am sure, now I think of it, that people will stop buying her goods. And where might that lead? I imagined her at home, with five hungry children to feed, and nothing to give them but sour milk.

18th September

This morning I watched as the herald stood outside by the gates, waiting to mount his horse. He was stuffing my letter into his bag on the flank of the animal. He stopped and chatted a moment with Matthew the groomsman. It was a sunny day, and he seemingly didn't see the need to follow my directions not to dally on the way.

A young girl I had never seen before came out from behind the chapel, holding a posy of wildflowers. I watched, horrified at first and then with an awe which surprised me, at how the girl skillfully pickpocketed my letter, swapping it for another. When the herald turned back and saw her standing there, she smiled and offered him the flowers, my original letter behind her back, her face a picture of innocence.

I flattened myself against the stone. What had I written that my enemies might pounce on? All they would know is my suspicions that Gravenor is connected to Richmond, and that was likely known to most. It would simply tell them how friendless and ignorant I am. But I wonder, perhaps them thinking that might make it easier to dupe them?

And now I knew one of their spies. That was an advantage to me, as was knowing that whatever message came back to me purporting to be from Wolsey would be a forgery. I could just call the guards and have the girl brought to me, of course. But I feel seeing what happens next could be even more helpful. To find out who these players are, I must let them play.

21st September

I was very excited today as we packed for the short journey to Tewkesbury Manor in the grounds of the town's abbey. For a little while, we think until the new year at least, this will be home. It takes us nearer our eventual goal too. I cannot believe we left London over a month ago and because of the building work and the dratted plague, we still haven't made it to the seat of power at Ludlow Castle.

"Do you think we shall ever reach Ludlow?" I asked Lady Margaret wearily.

She looked very strange, rather pale.

"Oh. Ludlow is a little way off yet. Maybe thirty miles or so from Tewkesbury, and we must be careful to protect you, Your Highness."

"Protect me?"

"Hmmm?" she was gazing out of the casement. There is something about Ludlow that bothers her.

"From the plague, you mean?"

"Yes, yes… from the sickness."

She snapped back into the room and smiled wanly. I do not have time to question her further, nor do I wish to right now. I have other things to ponder. Richmond and Gravenor are much on my mind. I must find a way to beat them and become my father's favourite. Otherwise, should both the Emperor and the French king shun me, I shall never wear a crown.

23rd September

Tewkesbury is a very fine and comfortable place. The manor house will be home for a while, and I am glad we can unpack my musical instruments and trunks and relax for a while.

When I returned from holding court in the Great Hall, I was handed a letter supposedly from Wolsey. I know of course that it is not. They have gone to great trouble to fake his wax seal. I noticed Gravenor watch carefully as I examined it, and smile to himself. How pleased he is to think he has tricked me! Ha! The letter read:

"Dear God-daughter,

I hope that this letter finds you well and free of the plague, which seems to constantly circle around you. (An attempt to frighten me, for the plague is no worse here than in London, and Wolsey wouldn't dream of causing me anxiety.)

I apologise that this letter is not in my hand, but I have incurred a slight wound whilst hunting (Wolsey rarely hunts) *and have had to defer to my scribe.* (Wolsey would never use a scribe. I swear he would write with his own feet if he had to.)

The problem must be solved of course, and though I have no intelligence to send you, I will have someone come to you to be of aid in this matter.

So that you know this person is from me, they will use the code word "endeavour" on being first presented at court. You must remember this and mark it well, Mary. (Wolsey is not so foolish as to use my first name in such a missive.) *Take this person into your confidence and they will help you in every matter. Never mind if they are young, they are entirely trustworthy.*

God bless you,

Wolsey."

The signature was fairly convincing but with rather too much flourish. I must watch out then, for a youngster who will use the word "endeavour." Then I shall know I have a spy in my midst.

25th September

"Shall we hunt today, Madam?" Lady Catherine asked, as the ladies began to dress me.

"Yes, why not? The men are restless, it might do them good to get the smell of blood in their nostrils and let off some steam."

She nodded at one of the girls, who went off to inform the steward, Lord Ferrers. Lord Ferret, I called him in my head, not so much for his looks, but because he always had his nose in everything. Part of his job, I suppose, to know what is going on.

Not that much is going on. No spy has turned up yet. I hate waiting for things. The travelling has been tiresome and annoying. Stopping for one night here, two more there. I am glad we have a base for a while, but one still cannot find everything since so much has been packed away. I miss my old rooms, my tapestries that lined the walls like familiar friends with their biblical scenes, the gardens where I knew every rose bush and tree. I miss Guinevere and my parents. They seem so far away and I so alone and unsure of myself. I have guides of course, to whom I am entrusted. Father leaves nothing to chance. My Lady Margaret is like a mother to me. But can I trust Lady Catherine and all these young ladies? Dudley, I trust, and my teachers, but what of these new lords?

I must remember what Hedges said. I need to remember who the falcon is. Let them circle, show themselves and their intentions, yet keep my own close to my heart. I thought a hunt a good way to see what is what, and who is who. But I learnt less about them and more about myself by the day's end.

The horses were fractious, eager to get going, for they too had been bored by recent events, or the lack of them.

"We shall hunt in the river, if it please Your Highness," said a nobleman I did not know. I thought his tone insolent, but he bowed his head and doffed his cap just a little as he spoke. His rich velvet robes could not hide the fact that he was rather round, and I pitied his horse.

I looked round in alarm at Dudley.

"Are we fishing or hunting? And who is this?"

"I beg your pardon, Your Highness," drawled Dudley. "I have not yet introduced you to Lord Puce. He owns Finchley Manor," he added, waving his hand disparagingly, "some small estate or other nearby. He will be hosting us today."

Lord Puce's face reddened. His colour and name were well matched.

"My estate... is um, many hundreds of acres, Your Highness. My lands are known for their richness and are very well-stocked."

"Then why, pray, should we need to go to your rivers?" I asked.

"Your Highness has but a small mare, and the otters will be easier to catch than my fine stags!"

"I see," I said coldly.

The hunting party trotted down to the river, which to be honest, was not much more than a wide stream. The weather was fine, and the water sparkled. I wondered if any otters would be found to hunt. They are notoriously fast and sleek, unlike Lord Puce.

Spears were thrown, most only finding water. A few sorry salmon and a couple of beavers were triumphantly spiked and then carried away as trophies. I found it unkind and unsporting. Beneath me – in every sense. Of course, for some of the party, it was an equal battle of wits. Then the ever-reddened Puce showed his inner colour.

"This one will do," he snarled, his spear pointed at a mother otter, nestled in the riverbank, nursing two cubs.

"Let her go," I said loudly. "Not fair game, that one."

"Agreed," Dudley said. But Puce wasn't listening to reason. He took deadly aim. The poor creature did not stand a chance.

I found myself leaping down from Sheba's back, and almost falling over my gown to reach the river. A stream of blood was flowing from the dying mother and one of the cubs had already floated away. The other was cradled, blood-stained, to its mother.

"Mary! Princess Mary! What are you doing?" called Dudley, dismounting with a leap.

I paid no heed; I was too busy wading into the water. I grabbed the mother and her small charge. In her last moments, with her fading eyes, she implored me to save her cub. I wanted to stand there and sob at the cruelty of it all, but I felt the pull of the water and knew I had to get back to the bank or I too could go the way of the other cub.

I struck out the way I had come, clutching the wretched creatures in the one arm, stumbling through tears and dragged down by my heavy dress. Dudley pulled me towards him with his strong arms. He brought me up onto the bank as Lord Puce came blundering along. The cowardly fiend took the mother from me, but I managed to cling on to the tiny cub.

"Give her back!" I screamed. "Give her back to me!"

The mother, I could see, was now dead, her head folded over onto her chest.

"Highness, whatever is the matter with you?" Puce said, taking no trouble to hide his disgust. "Why should you want the rat?"

I felt hot with rage. I was about to shriek at him when Dudley turned my face to his.

"Your Highness. You must focus. We must get you back to your ladies and get you dry."

I kept my eyes on his face as he held onto me. No-one tried to take the small animal from me. I held it tight to my chest as we cantered back to the manor, dispensing with convention and etiquette with Dudley holding me tight and true upon his steed.

Everything was a blur after that. I remember that I would not let go of the tiny otter cub and that it was only Lady Margaret promising to take care of it that made me part with it. I don't think I knew what danger I was in, or how delirious the chill had already made me. But God bless her, she kept her word and handed the little soul back to me once I was tucked up in a thick cotton nightdress in my bed, warmed gently by a copper pan full of hot coals.

The apothecary was called. He was a young man with sweaty hands. I did not like him much. I let him feel my forehead and listen to my heart. He gave the ladies a tincture for me and said that they must keep a watch on my temperature. If I didn't steady by nightfall, he would bring leeches to bleed me with. That brought me back to myself, I think. I hate leeches.

It was only then that I gave the creature my full attention. He was not so bedraggled as before. Lady Margaret had washed him free of his mother's blood, dried him and wrapped him in a small blanket before handing him back to me. He had the dearest little face. He licked my finger and then fell fast asleep. As, very soon, did I.

26th September

Fortunately, on waking I felt fine and did not have any signs of fever, doubtless thanks to Dudley's quick actions. I will make sure when I next write to Father to say that he has taken good care of me. I will not let on how stupid I was launching myself out into cold water just to save a small animal though.

Last night, I had a strange dream which I have only remembered now as I come to write. It makes me shudder to think on it. I was hunting, my entourage and I throwing spears into the river. We were laughing as we hit our marks, which were not otters, beavers or any kind of animal. They were people. The river was full of the dead and wounded, and it was streaming with blood. That was not the worst thing though. The worst thing was that I enjoyed it. That truly shocked me.

Lancelot, the otter, has settled in quite well. Matthew has made him a little run in the hallway with a long trough of water that he can play in. He has turned out to be a she, however, so I have decided to call her Lottie. This made Lizzie Pole laugh.

"Lottie Otter!" she said.

Sometimes her silliness is sweet. Lottie is too. She does take a little milk, but I hope soon to see salmon on her menu. I have ordered some extra to be fished and asked for it to come from Lord Puce's estate. I want him to pay dearly for his cruelty and rudeness.

30th September

I have been on tenterhooks waiting for the spy to show. I expected every person under the age of 30 who came to me with a petition or problem yesterday to say "endeavour." Indeed, I was listening so hard for it I had to ask a few of them to repeat their requests. Then, just as I was wondering what we might be having for lunch, a girl, all a jitter, came in. She looked as though she'd been pushed from the sidelines.

"Errrr," she said. Not an inspiring beginning.

"Yes, young girl, what is it you need?" I said graciously, trying to pretend I'd never seen her before.

"Your Highness, I come to you with a will to be of service. My family have thrown me out because I was schooling myself with letters. I heard that the Princess learns Latin and French and is very clever."

She bit her lip then, as if trying to remember what she'd been told to say.

"I thought you might take pity on me, and if you take me on, I shall *endeavour* to serve you with all my heart and soul, Your Highness."

She stressed the word "endeavour" so hard that I had trouble not laughing. If this was the best my enemies could offer, I have little to fear from them.

"What is your name, child?" I asked the girl, a little older than I.

"Clara, Your Highness."

She curtsied. Quite badly.

"Well, Clara. The first thing we shall do is have you taught how to curtsy properly."

The court and bystanders all laughed, gently. The girl

was meant to seem utterly harmless. Guileless, perhaps. I would remain on my guard. Seeming something is not the same as being something.

5th October

Clara's sweetness is making my blood boil. She fawns over everyone and smiles in a way that seems totally false to me. I wonder that no-one sees through her deception. I've been watching her carefully, and I see that when she thinks she is not being watched, her face is sullen. She is far from the angel she appears.

I am glad I know this and cannot be fooled. I wonder if I ought to take anyone else into my confidence, or whether that might stop me finding out who put her in place. Whom might I trust? Dudley perhaps? Lady Catherine? Lady Margaret, I trust implicitly of course, but she is too soft for subterfuge. I will think on it.

We had a gloriously entertaining morning with Lottie today. She raced up and down in her water-run, splashing everyone in sight. I am so glad I rescued her. She brings much joy.

6th October

Oh, how wrong I was about Lottie. Last night I took to my bed full of the joy she brings, but this morning I have only hatred towards her. When I woke, I thought to stroke her soft belly, but she clawed my hand! She only drew a little blood, so I did not call anyone, but I am cross with myself for allowing myself to be fooled into thinking a wild animal could be any kind of pet or could show me affection. I will now have to find a way to get rid of it without looking heartless, or worse, foolish.

9th October

Fortunately, the increasingly tiresome Clara found a way for me to do what was necessary. She was already annoying me with her cloying ways, but today she really upset me. She was playing too boisterously with Lottie and getting the little otter over-excited. I was still trying to be careful around the spy and working out what pretenses and false information I might send back to her masters through her. But for the moment it seemed her job was less about gathering clues than being just plain bothersome.

"If you keep doing that, you'll regret it," Cecily said, quite rightly. "You must be gentle."

Two minutes later there was a yelp from the foolish girl. I was quite pleased but took care not to show it.

"My finger! I've lost my finger! It bit off my finger!" she screamed, blood staining the rugs below.

She went to hit the otter, but Lizzie pulled her away.

"How dare you!" I shouted. "You would hit a poor defenceless creature? The Princess's pet! My sweet Lottie!"

My ladies were surprised, no doubt, at how strongly they imagined I felt. But I was mostly upset about having been too soft-hearted. I shall not make any kind of queen, let alone a good one, if I go wading into rivers to rescue small animals who turn on me. Also, I was frustrated with Clara and her underhand ways.

"Look!" she said in response, and certainly, the tip of her left index finger was missing. Lottie was chewing on it quite happily in fact.

"Well, take the tiresome child to the apothecary, then," I said to the other girls. "Have her bandaged and soothed."

"But, my finger!" the girl sobbed.

"Oh, hush with your complaining. You brought it completely on yourself. And it's not like you were going to learn the lute, is it? Or master the harpsichord?"

Clara was open-mouthed, Lizzie looked shocked, and Cecily nearly spat out her drink.

This afternoon things were taken out of my hands. Biting the feckless Clara had redeemed Lottie in my eyes and now I was reluctant, once more, to lose her. However, Lord Ferrers came to see me and said that he could not sanction keeping such a dangerous animal so close to me.

"It has had a taste of human flesh, now, Your Highness. What if it bit you? Or gave you some dreadful disease? No, I am afraid the creature must be taken back to the river."

"That's not fair! Lottie was provoked. She wouldn't hurt me!" I yelled, hoping my face wouldn't reveal my lie.

"I'm sorry, Your Highness. Clara came to us, and Dudley and I are quite one mind on this."

A little wave of compassion came over me, and I covered the small scratch on my hand as I spoke.

"But she has never had to fend for herself, she is far too small and would die!"

Lady Margaret was with us and sought, as she always does, to find a diplomatic solution.

"It was Matthew, wasn't it, Your Highness, who made Lottie this run?" I nodded. "Perhaps it might be acceptable to all if Lottie were to stay with him out in the stables. She could have her run there and you might visit."

"Matthew could teach her how to fish!" said Lizzie. "He is so good with animals."

And so, it was decided. Despite everything, I wish Lottie well. She should never have been brought inside. Wild things do not make good pets. As for Clara, she has lost a fingertip and helped me save face. Perhaps her stupidity will serve me again.

12th October

I decided to go back to the market in Gloucester today. It was nice to see the commoners bow and scrape, doffing their caps, averting their gaze from mine. I must ensure the people love me if I am to be more popular than Richmond. Father will not care so much what the northerners think of my half-brother, he never listens to those beyond London, but he must hear good reports of me from the people here.

As I'd hoped, the troupe performing the Arthurian legends were still there in the heart of the town square. They were acting out a battle of magics between Morgana and Merlin. We stayed quiet at the back for now. I wanted to watch.

"I shall strike you with my evil wand!" cried the young teenage boy playing the witch. His blond wig was ill-fitting, all lopsided, a bit like his grin.

"That's not what it says in the script," boomed a voice from the cart next to the makeshift stage. "Get it right!"

The audience laughed. The teenage boy's shoulders slumped. The troupe had not yet seen their royal visitor.

"I can't remember all them fancy words!" he sighed.

"It's not hard. Marry, lad. I'll do it for ye," and out came the large, jovial man who had played King Arthur on my procession day. He first grabbed the boy's wig and put it atop his own pate, making the crowd laugh even more, then took the wand.

"Today you shall become an evil toad spectre, by the power of my birch stick, soaked in the blood of my most virtuous enemies!" he said, lunging forwards towards the old man playing Merlin with the wand, as though it were a sword.

Merlin shrieked and took a step back. Again, laughter. The boy shrugged.

"It's too much to keep in my head Mister Shakespeare, much too much!"

"Too much ado about nothing!" said the older man. "The playwright worked late at night to get the words right, least ye could do is match 'em."

I beckoned Dudley over.

"I want this troupe for the revels, Dudley. I especially want this large man to be there. He is very entertaining." I pointed at the Shakespeare chap. "I like the way he speaks."

"As you wish, Your Highness," said Dudley.

In truth, the man reminded me of Father, so full of life and confidence, not like the conniving dullards I am so often surrounded by. A man of integrity and passion with a gift for storytelling, just what is needed to liven up Christmas.

"I bid thee welcome!" said the actor.

The crowd, now aware of my presence, parted to allow our horses passage to the stage.

"We have company for our company! Royalty no less!"

40

and the man bowed down with a great flourish, whipping his large, feathered hat off with one arm and spreading out the other.

The younger man whimpered and ran off the stage, and Merlin did likewise on the other side. I decided to test the man's arrogance and his wit. We trotted our horses forward.

"Your Highness is most welcome to our humble entertainments," the large man continued, remaining on bended knee.

"I thank ye," I said calmly. "And whom might one be addressing?"

"My name is Richard Shakespeare, Highness."

"You now appear to be a company of one, Mister Shakespeare."

I saw him grin. Or perhaps he was grimacing; he may have been in pain kneeling at his age. He must be at least thirty.

"You may rise."

"Oh, thank you kindly, Madam. I am afraid my fellows have become shy and very much in awe of Your Highness' presence."

"They are doubtless tongue-tied, Mister Shakespeare."

"Indeed, my lady."

"Not an affliction that often bothers you, I'll be bound."

The crowd laughed.

"The words seem to tumble out of their own accord, Your Highness."

I looked beyond Shakespeare at the jester, who, much to my horror, was prancing towards me.

"Well met, like acrobats, falling and jumping!" cried the jester, "the actors pour watery words out of their very mouths and make worlds out of nothing but thin air!"

Mister Shakespeare rolled his eyes.

"And you are not the only one who has difficulty being quiet, it seems," I sighed.

"True, Your Highness. But a good performer knows the power of silence too, when warranted."

And then, I am quite sure, the upstart actor winked at me. At me, the Princess of Wales! I was too amazed to take offence.

"And of those times, your Royal Highness, when actions speak louder than words."

He raced over to the jester, clapped both hands around his ears and kissed him full on the lips. The crowd laughed loudly. The jester spluttered and pulled away, falling backwards over a firkin of beer, and Mister Shakespeare pointed Merlin's wand at the beleaguered man, threatening him with a curse.

"Begone foul fiend!" he said, "Take your bells and wittering elsewhere!"

And as the jester turned round to try to get up, my new friend made a show of kicking him in the rear. The crowd roared and cheered. I could not stop laughing. Indeed, I find myself giggling anew as I write this account!

13th October

I forgot to write about meeting Hazel yesterday at the market. I was so taken with Mister Richard Shakespeare's antics that, until now, it had slipped my mind.

There were many children frolicking around the cheese-seller's stall. The tiniest of the many wore a little smock and had his thumb in his mouth as he tucked himself into the folds of his mother's skirt. There were a few more girls dancing on the green with ribbons. Most unladylike.

"Are these *all* yours?" I asked.

The woman coloured a little and lowered her head.

"Only *five*, Your Highness. These three boys. One of my girls is on the green and Hazel is here, helping her mother as usual. A good girl."

She curtsied.

I turned to Hazel, who was helping lay out the stall. I almost gasped when she looked up at me. It was like looking in a mirror. The girl's face was the exact thin oval as mine, with the same blue eyes shining back at me. She even had the same shaped nose, and was staring at me defiantly, as if she truly was my equal. I made up my mind there and then to knock that out of her. And yet. I wondered if she might come in useful.

"You will come to the castle. You will be my playmate." I commanded.

I nodded at the woman behind the table of cheeses, who had gone as pale as her wares.

"Your mother will be paid."

The girl looked round in a panic. Her mother avoided her gaze and curtsied.

"Pack your things, Hazel."

25th October

The new girl, Hazel, keeps crying. She is missing her mother perhaps. But I am not crying, and mine is much further away. Perhaps it is hard to always be preparing feasts, and never partaking of them. But then, as Lady Margaret would say, that is what servants are for.

"You are always ascribing feelings to people, Mary," she said, when I had remarked upon the servants' grim faces after church. "You cannot know another's heart. Or head. These simple souls are likely just bored. They cannot understand the Dean's sermons!"

I said nothing in reply, for Dean Wooton's sermons make me want to sleep. I envy the other children allowed to nod off in the back rows. I, of course, have all eyes on me when sat in the royal pew. Sometimes I wish I could be more like Father. At Westminster, the Cardinal sometimes had to shout to be heard over his snores.

"What?" he said to my mother as she chided him once. "I'm the King! I may do as I please! I'm tired from the hunt yesterday. The Sabbath day was made for resting, wasn't it? Then I shall rest! Best time to do such holy work, in Church, if you ask me."

I remember he turned and winked at me, even as the Queen shook her head. It makes me weep a little now, to think of them. They seem so far away. I wonder when I shall see them again.

31st October

I was looking out of the window today during Latin. Dr Fetherstone told me to pay attention, but I really didn't want to. It was a bright, sunny day, just right for riding.

"We promised your mother to finish learning these irregular verbs this week, Highness," he said with pursed lips.

He always brings Mother into it when I'm not doing what he wants. I think it's mean. I wish she weren't so interested in my Latin. It's not like anyone's going to mark my work when I'm an Empress or Queen of all England. But we have to send her some of my exercises now and then. In Spanish too, though I don't mind that so much. The French is easy now, so I don't really have to work too hard.

I sighed as I spotted Hazel and Lizzie outside walking. I know my ladies work hard, but the younger ones don't have too much to do. I wonder if I should make them have lessons. I do wish I could change places with them sometimes.

"Yes, Dr Fetherstone," I said, and then I told the good doctor that I had a headache and he excused me.

I ought to be able to excuse *him*, but alas, even princesses must be schooled. Time, perhaps I started doing some schooling of my own. Of Puce and Gravenor for starters. They ought to learn some lessons in how to treat a future monarch, that's for sure!

Without her knowing, I have been schooling Hazel too. Soon she will have been here long enough. She will know enough of the way of things and enough about me to be passed off as me. If we dressed in each other's clothes, would anyone really notice? My heart is pounding at the thought of doing something so daring. I won't be able to sleep tonight for planning how to carry it out!

4th November

Hazel and I have it all planned out! She is ready. Tomorrow

she is going to creep into my room, and we will change clothes. I into her dress and she into my nightgown.

"But what if they realise, Highness? I would be in such trouble! Would they chop off my head?" the soon-to-be princess asked.

"Silly! I am the one in charge of chopping off people's heads. This whole thing was my idea. Who am I going to get in trouble with? The most I will get is a lecture from Lady Catherine, or a hard stare from Lady Margaret! You know I have them wound around my finger like thread. Don't worry. It will be fun!"

"I'm not sure doing your Latin exercises will be fun."

"Ha! No. But that's why I'll pay your mother an extra half-crown a week."

"Half a crown? Really? Oh, that's splendid! Thank you."

"Every week this plan works, that is, Hazel. So do your best for me and for your mother, alright? Now let's practice again. You practice how I walk, and I will practice how you sound. It is so hard to speak like a peasant."

She chewed her lip, which meant she wanted to say something. But I ignored her. True, she doesn't really know any Latin, and so she'll have to face Dr Fetherstone's wrath, and her French is non-existent. But Professor Duwes mostly reads his own books during lesson time and writes them too, leaving me, or in this case, a pretend me, to get on with exercises, so I can always correct Hazel's work later. What a lark for me to be outside playing, laughing and riding, and poor Hazel stuck in doing my lessons. Half a crown well-spent I say!

5th November

Everything went perfectly today! Dressed in Hazel's clothes, I left my own chambers and then returned to find my ladies performing her toilette and dressing her for the schoolroom. It was all I could do to stop myself bursting out laughing. I didn't dare even catch Hazel's eye. Instead, with head bowed, I asked the 'Princess' if I might go outside and play today.

"Of course, you may, Hazel," she said, grandly. "It is sunny today and you have been looking very pale recently. Get some sun."

I curtsied, afforded myself an inner smile, and took my leave.

Despite being so late in the year, it was a gloriously sunny day, and I ran about here, there and everywhere like a hungry hare. I walked along the river, watched the minnows from the shade, and even sat on a log and dabbled my bare feet into the cooling water. Lady Catherine would never have let me do that! I walked barefoot back to the apartments, dangling my hard shoes from one hand. I am not used to wearing wooden clogs, so I do have a few blisters now. But it was wonderful to feel the grass on my skin. I wonder how I shall manage to get away and ride? I cast an upwards glance at the leaded window of the classroom, but I did not feel guilty. If a princess can't have any freedom at all, what is the point in being one?

I did find my heart beating very loudly as I headed back indoors. What if my double had been discovered? I needn't have worried. Hazel is a very fine actor as it turns out. Mister Shakespeare would do well to have her in his company, if girls were allowed that is. Honestly, there is so much we are not supposed to do!

"Oh, Your Highness," my collaborator told me as we swapped clothes before dinner. "It was so boring. How do you sit there and listen to Dr Fetherstone going on and on about tense endings? I thought I would go quite mad."

"It is awful, isn't it? I am sorry. But oh, it was so delicious to be outside!"

She scowled slightly, and probably thought better of speaking her mind, showing the restraint of a princess.

"It was nice not to have to help carry laundry and to wear such beautiful clothes!" she explained, once her scowl had fallen.

"I think we should only do this once in a while. Let us see if anyone questions us about today, and then we can plan what to do next! I should like to go riding on my own."

She screwed up her face in concentration: "Well, being bad at languages might give me away. And if they ask me to play the spinet…"

"You'll have to refuse for now! Or learn."

I thought about that. Perhaps I can teach Hazel more things. It would help if she were as much like me as possible. For now, we shall be cautious and continue as normal perhaps until after Christmas. Right now, it is time to get some rest, for the fresh air has made me sleepy.

13th November

Today we were treated to a wonderful pageant by Shakespeare's troupe. Mister Shakespeare made a most belligerent Sheriff, and both Robin Hood and Maid Marion were played by young lads with voices that were constantly going up and down. I'm not sure that was meant to be funny, but it was, nevertheless.

"You are miserable wretches, and I shall eat your cold hearts for breakfast!" shouted the Sheriff near the end, before adding, "with grated cheese and a pickled egg!"

We all laughed and if I'm honest, I'm fairly sure that I was not the only one who secretly wanted the wicked ruler to win. But Robin got the girl and the treasure, as always happens. I was surrounded by all my courtiers to watch the performance and thought I might sow a few seeds of make-believe into the mix myself.

"How is your finger, my dear?" I whispered to Clara, who was sat to my left.

She nodded and showed me how it was healing, which was well, thankfully.

"You know, I am not so keen on all these plays and schemes. I much prefer to ride. In that," I continued, "I suppose I am much like my father, and my half-brother too."

You could almost see her ears prick up, like a chubby cat's.

"I hear that he is not so popular in the north as I am here, and I am sorry for him. But I think mostly my people love me for my straight-talking. I don't understand it when people scheme and plot."

"Indeed, Your Highness," she said, lapping up every word.

Far better that my enemies think me an innocent.

"These Lords, for instance," I said nodding surreptitiously at Puce and Gravenor, who were, as always, sat together at the side of the hall. "You might tell me, some time, Clara, indeed you might *endeavour* to tell me what they are up to. That would be a help. I cannot make head or tail of them and their ways."

She smiled knowingly.

"Indeed, madam, I shall do my very best."

I smile now as I prepare for bed. For she is the fly, and I am the spider, and she is stuck in my invisible web – not I in hers.

Christmas Eve

The court convened very late tonight. We had left many things unresolved because of all the preparations for Christmas, and I was told it was traditional to hold a meeting for petitioners and the landowners after dinner this night, just before Midnight Mass in the chapel.

Mostly, it was business as usual and unspeakably boring. The highlight was the matter of a prize cow that had taken a liking to a neighbouring farmer's field, leading him to claim ownership of her. I pronounced the rights of the actual owner but told him he must pay grazing fees to the other if he could not keep his cow from wandering off. The people clapped my wisdom.

The proceedings may have been dull, but the great hall was anything but, looking magical draped with holly and ivy, the bright berries glinting ruby-red in the glow of candlelight.

Permissions for burial followed before someone asked for my seal of approval on their wares, which I gave, since on Christmas Eve it would have been churlish not to. It was now only half an hour till midnight, and then Christmas could begin!

"Well, we are near the blessed hour!" I pronounced. "Is there any other urgent business that cannot wait until the festivities are over?"

"Oh, I think I have something which needs dealing with immediately," drawled Gravenor.

His voice was ice-cold, and he sounded as though he were bored and had something immensely more important to go and deal with.

"Oh yes, Lord…" pretending to forget his name.

"Gravenor," said Ferrers.

"Oh, of course."

"I have discovered that there is a sheep rustler taking ewes from my land and smuggling them over the border into Shropshire."

"I'm sorry to hear that. Are you here to bring charges?"

"I am. The miscreant stands in this very room and must be punished most severely."

"I will be the judge of that," I said.

Two could play at being cold. He shrugged.

"Where is this supposed villain and where is your proof, Gravenor?"

"I have several witnesses, Your Highness, who have signed statements."

This meant nothing, since Gravenor would force signatures out of his tenants with threats as we had discovered he had done before. The farmer who had come to us at the very first court we held here was vindicated and given a good settlement of monies. Gravenor had been itching for revenge ever since.

"And the villain is Mister Richard Shakespeare of Bell

Lane, Snitterfield"

There was an uproar. Mister Shakespeare was well-liked as his company were often here to entertain us. I bit my lip. Perhaps I had put him in danger by making it so clear he held my favour.

"The accused shall approach the throne," I said, trying to keep my composure.

"Your Highness!" protested Shakespeare. "I am innocent! As innocent as a new-born lamb!"

He was bundled forward by Gravenor's henchmen.

"Ha!" shouted Puce, wanting to join in. "You are a scoundrel and a low-life!"

"Better than being a milksop poltroon!" Shakespeare shouted back.

I do love how he insults people! But what was I to do? Mister Shakespeare could be guilty, but likelier still that Gravenor just trumped this up to put me in a difficult position. He wants me to ruin Christmas and have all the people hate me.

I like Mister Shakespeare, and I believe him to be a loyal subject. He is almost a friend, if a princess can have friends. But how could I get him out of his punishment and show Puce and Gravenor that I am a proper ruler? I felt so lost. All I could see in my head was poor Mister Shakespeare laid out in the stocks, his back breaking and all the children pelting him with rotten tomatoes. Then, I realised that Dudley was coughing close by my ear.

"Your Highness. Before we continue with this case, I do have a small point of order that needs addressing."

I would have been cross with him for interrupting my thoughts, except that he had one perfectly curved eyebrow raised, which meant I should take note of what he was saying.

"Yes, Dudley, what is it?" I answered, feigning annoyance. "You know not to interrupt my court."

"Apologies, Highness, but it is almost midnight, and Your Highness has yet to appoint a Lord of Misrule. The peasants are getting quite restless over it."

I frowned in thought. The Lord of Misrule is a commoner who would make the rules as a pretend king all over the Christmas season. It was a bit of fun, but a very important way to show everyone what the people really thought about their leaders. He would take charge of feasts and organise entertainments, as well as having some small powers like being able to pardon minor misdemeanors in a mock court.

That was it! If I made Mister Shakespeare the Lord of Misrule for the twelve nights of Christmas, he could pardon himself! He certainly wouldn't be able to be punished! I laughed and smiled at Lord Gravenor in a way he clearly did not like.

"Oh well, I suppose there is only one candidate to manage the revels this year, Dudley. It must be Mister Shakespeare, of course!"

Richard stood up straight. Until now, he'd been looking decidedly sorry for himself.

"Oh, Your Highness, but that would mean that this court must be adjourned, surely, until after Christmas?" said my trusted advisor.

"Oh no, Dudley," I countered, surprising him with a grin. "I see no occasion for that. Since there is no way to counter Lord Gravenor's witness statements, let us give Mister Shakespeare the appropriate punishment."

The clock began to strike midnight.

Richard's face fell again, and Gravenor's brightened.

Dudley merely looked bemused.

"He should clearly spend one afternoon in the village stocks and two days in gaol."

The public gallery was outraged. But the booing did not last long, as they saw I was about to speak again.

"And now, I hand proceedings over to Mister Shakespeare, Lord of Misrule, Master of the Revels, to proceed with any other small legal matters, pardons and so on, before he begins the important business of organising Christmas."

The crowd did not know whether to boo or cheer.

Mister Shakespeare was brought up to the throne, which I relinquished for him, with a curtsey. I even gave him the small sceptre that lay against the gilded chair.

He whispered to me urgently: "Did Your Highness say pardons?"

"I did," I smiled.

He grinned.

Mister Richard Shakespeare, the Lord of Misrule, sat on his throne and grinned some more, the royal sceptre in one hand and a tankard of mulled wine in the other. He looked decidedly comfortable. A little too much, perhaps! But I folded my arms and played along and shook my head at him, and all the commoners and courtiers laughed. All except one. Gravenor was staring at me and then at the interloper through squinted eyes.

"My first ruling, in this court, as Lord of Misrule," pronounced Mister Shakespeare loudly, on the last stroke of midnight, and the first moment of Christmas, "is to pardon the reprobate accused sheep rustler and all-round good egg, as well as superb actor, Mister Richard Shakespeare!"

The crowd roared with laughter.

"Well, bless my soul, that be me!" he continued.

Tankards were raised as he continued. In the spirit of the moment, and buoyed by all the raucous laughter, I'm afraid I could not resist poking my tongue out at Gravenor. He was furious! But the people cheered loudly.

"And my second, is a wish that you all have a Merry Christmas and more spiced ale from the kitchens!"

The Great Hall quickly turned from a courtroom to a feast. Gravenor glared daggers at me before disappearing with Puce and his other pitiful accomplices. I have won this battle, but I fear he will go to greater and greater lengths to hurt me and to ruin my chances of becoming Queen.

Christmas Day

Perhaps unsurprisingly, most people were quite subdued at the church service this morning. A record amount of ale and wine, not to mention some of the food meant for today, had been consumed during the night. More than a few heads were spinning. Of course, as a princess, and yet a child, I had gone to Midnight Mass before retiring, and left the revellers to it.

The Lord of Misrule looked a little paler than usual, sat at the back. As I walked past to take my seat in the royal pew, I could tell his laurel crown was wilting a bit. I wonder what he will be like on the twelfth night if this is the state of him after the first!

28th December

My goodness, how we are feasting! I have never seen so many wild boars roasted with apples in their mouths! Father would be most envious. He loves wild boar. He is a bit like one himself, the way his temper is and how he charges around. Mind you, I'd like to see the man who could put an apple in his mouth!

Mister Shakespeare has outdone himself as the Lord of Misrule and Master of Ceremonies. We have had plays and pageants, singing and dancing, with musicians brought in from five counties. It has been one long party.

He says that there is one very special surprise that he is saving for New Year's Day. Everyone is talking about what it might be. I think a new play, but Lizzie and Cecily tell me that there have been a number of carpenters hard at work in the work sheds. I wonder what they are making.

It does feel good not to have to do lessons. I have allowed Hazel and some of the local servants home for a few days so that they can celebrate Christmas with family. Hazel went with a few extra coins in her pocket for her mother, and instructions to bring back some fine cheeses. I hope now that I have made it up with her family, but also, I believe that we are friends, at least of a sort. Shared secrets will do that. I am still amazed that no-one else has seen the similarity between us. I suppose more people judge by clothing than you would think.

1526

1st January

Well! I can hardly believe what happened tonight! After dinner and plenty of libations, we were all sat in great expectations of what Mister Shakespeare had planned. I was on my throne, a circlet of gold encrusted with pearls on my head, feeling more like a ruler and a true princess than I have for a very long time. I wore my russet velvet gown with the pearled stomacher and knew I looked very regal. But what was I presiding over today? The usual straw on the floor had been swept up and the long wooden benches pushed to the sides and laid upon it were squares of black and white.

"Is Your Highness ready to do battle?" called a familiar voice from the corridor.

"Against whom?" I called back.

"Against the fiendish Spaniards!" Shakespeare shouted. "The yellow-bellied armada of the King of Spain!"

Everyone laughed. This might have been risky since my own mother was Spanish but given that it was now public knowledge that Charles was to marry Isabella of Portugal, I had few worries about wanting to trounce him and his rotten navy!

"Those curved-hatted rats shall drown in the channel!" I yelled with all my might.

The door was flung wide, and in strode a company of boats to great cheers. A veritable flotilla! Here were ten of my serving lads, including Matthew the stable hand, in white shirts and hose, with wooden ships built around their midriffs! Everyone oohed and aahed at the cleverness of it.

The ships were well carved, with little pieces of rigging and model cannons on their flanks. The young men looked embarrassed to have prows and sterns made of wood, but in truth they looked splendid. Their white shirts bore the Tudor Rose, and their hats had green ribbons tied to them to complete the ensign. They each had a leather pouch slung around their necks, their contents and purpose yet to be revealed.

"The English navy patrol the King's shores with courage!" called Richard, as the boats bobbed up and down and sailed around one another. It was all so well planned! I almost felt seasick.

"But soft, what is this on the horizon? Here come the paltry, wicked Spanish pirates, wanting to loot our English treasures and land on our green and pleasant shores!"

The English navy roared and stomped their feet as the armada sailed into the room from the far end. The Spanish galleons were just as beautifully crafted as the English ones, but the men wearing them were a little older. Even Sir Ralph the Treasurer was there in a curved steel helmet, though I'm not sure he understood entirely what was happening. Their shirts were squares of red and white with the golden castles and red lions of Spain, and their helmets had red and gold ribbons flying from them. They looked very stately. But I had high hopes of the English winning the battle!

Each flotilla took it in turns to roll the gaming dice, to decide how many squares they could advance. The first English ship moved five squares towards the Spanish.

"You may fire your cannons!" yelled Mister Shakespeare

from the kitchen doorway.

The Englishman reached into his pouch and brought out three horse chestnuts. Expertly, and to much cheering, he also brought out a catapult and fired the conkers at the Spanish ships, tearing a hole into the port side of one. There was a great uproar from the Spaniards, who, it seemed, had not been issued with catapults. They started lobbing hazelnuts and sweet chestnuts back, and Mister Shakespeare had to shout at them to play fair.

There were a few more rounds of dice rolling and playing by the rules, but after that the whole thing descended into chaos, as battles doubtless do. I felt sorry for the poor carpenters. It was a good job they were not there to see their wonderful creations getting damaged by nuts and berries. One of the English boats was even using crabapples, which were devastating from a distance. Laughter and shouting soon turned to cursing and brawling. I was laughing so much I could not issue an order for them to stop. In the end Dudley and Ferrers had to send in guards to pull them all apart.

2nd January

Once the festivities are over, we are to move on to Worcester and finally stay with Prior More, who has been offering us hospitality from the beginning. I shall be sorry to leave Tewkesbury, which has become a home from home. But at least we are not very far and can visit. Matthew believes it will be kinder to return Lottie to the river here, rather than move her such a distance.

"She has learned fishing very well," he said proudly, as I

visited Sheba. "I take her down to the water most days. Lately, she has been less keen to come back to me."

I pretended to be a little sad, but to be honest here in my diary, I can say I'm glad. She taught me I can no longer be soft and that I cannot afford to give my heart away so easily.

"It's time to let her go then?" I asked, letting false tears catch in the corner of my eyes.

"You can say goodbye if you like, Your Highness."

I shook my head. That will be the last I'll see of my dear Lottie.

9th January

We are on the move again then. This time back to Worcester. A place nearer Ludlow Castle, called Hartlebury, will be made ready for us as a base when we leave here, but that will not be until the spring. How strange it is to have had so many different homes in a year! I thought I might get used to the upheaval, but I find I cannot. I want to make the people love me, and I can't do that if I'm forever on the move.

Two days ago, we were at Battenhall Manor and today, after yet more travelling, we were welcomed most graciously by our host in Worcester, Prior More. He seems a kind and gentle soul. Humbler than many clergymen. I liked him at once and hope he is someone I can trust. He could see I was tired and bade us eat and retire without too much talking. That was thoughtful.

I have been wondering what else to let slip to Clara. Perhaps it was a mistake not to have just had her arrested as soon as she stole the letter. All this plotting and scheming is a lot to hold in one's head. When she is about, I play the dim-witted card. I play at being softer-hearted and unable to cope with difficult things. This afternoon I pretended to cry about a family I have never met who have been hit hard by the plague. I am hoping that this sort of thing reported to them will mean the villain lords won't be expecting me to rise and fight my corner.

"You are soft, aren't you?" said Clara, the little traitor. "Especially when it comes to animals."

I thought she was talking about little Lottie, and still sore about her stupid finger.

20th January

We are settling in well now, and I like Worcester of course, knowing it already. It is a shame Ludlow is still such a way off. I don't really understand what is taking so long. Surely my father hadn't let it get into too much of a state of disrepair? I sometimes think this wandering about and staying in new places is all part of my trial.

I miss my parents very much. And the familiarity of Ditton. I had not expected home-sickness to pull so hard, nor be so fierce on my heart. I went to pray in the chapel this morning and Prior More walked in to find me sobbing on a prie-dieu. He asked me if I wanted to talk or be left alone, which was kind of him.

I know not to divulge anything to a stranger, but I did tell him I was missing home and he sat and prayed with me. I found this most comforting. He is very kind and seems genuine in his Christian faith and manners. But he is only a Prior and does not know much about affairs of state.

"Chapels can seem a little bare and dull once all the festivities are over," I said, trying to say something boring to pull myself out of painful emotions. The Prior looked thoughtful.

"I find, Your Highness, that a place full of holiness can never be dull."

He gazed up at the crucifix over the altar and then looked back at me and smiled. Something stirred in my heart. He is right I suppose. At least the church is a mother who will not forget me (my own does not write so often as she did) and God is a father who will not send me away.

14th February

The men hunted yesterday. I leave them to it mostly now. I know I'm supposed to enjoy it, but after the debacle with Lottie, I find I don't have the stomach for it. In any case, I'm not really tall enough yet. I much prefer archery. I can hunt hare and rabbit for the kitchens from a long way off now and I don't have to suffer their faces. How Father can enjoy bear-baiting I do not know.

I've heard tales of cock-fighting here at some of the inns. I shudder to think of it, though part of me would still like to see. Sometimes it seems all we do is kill things, or bay for their blood. How wicked we humans are! And yet, blood is so fascinating. It bonds us all. No wonder we want to see it. I confess, I am still having that nightmare about the river flowing with it. It vexes me, since I do not know what it means.

Today we had a dance for Valentines. I played the virginals to great applause. Lady Margaret and Lady Catherine agree that I am extremely talented. It is infuriating that the instruments are never quite perfectly in tune due to being moved about so much. But I will have them with me wherever we go, since music is one of the things that feeds my soul and helps me imagine a better world.

And then we drew lots for our Valentine's and the minstrels played up in the gallery for a dance. It was so much fun! We all sat round in a big circle, as though it were very serious. I decided to be playful.

"Now, be assured everyone, though we are allowing fate to play with our hearts, we must stay true to whoever is our Valentine today. We must dance with them, however bad their breath smells, however many warts they have on their nose, and however much they delight in wearing yellow garters."

Yellow garters are all the fashion with the men of court at the moment, but I think they look silly. Lord Ferrers was wearing them as I spoke and looked very embarrassed when everyone laughed.

A large red velvet bag containing all the gentlemen's names was passed around to all the ladies. It seems as sensible a way to choose a partner as any other. Men were slapped on the back and congratulated if they were chosen by one of my ladies in waiting, who are all young, and commiserated on receiving a married or older lady. As it came to my turn, there was a hush about the room. It would be a great honour to have me as a Valentine. I was hoping for Dudley, or one of the better dancers at least, and very much hoping against Puce or Gravenor. I did not

63

want to dance with one of my enemies. I pulled the scrap of paper out and unfolded it carefully, all eyes on me. I roared with laughter, before bringing myself under control.

"Well! Ladies, I am very sorry, but you will have to forgive me for getting the pick of the bunch this year. For I am partnered to the most elegant of Ireland's subduers, the Ranger of Delamere Forest."

There was a chatter and confusion from those who did not know whom I meant.

"Step forward for your Valentine's kiss, Sir Ralph!"

For my Valentine was none other than the elderly treasurer, Sir Ralph Egerton.

"Oh!" he said and dragged himself up to the old oak chair that passed here for a throne. He had trouble walking, for he was much affected by gout. His nose was red and puffed up, and he was at least seven times my age.

"Come, come, Sir Ralph. I am eager for you to teach me the ways of dance, and of love!"

Everyone laughed and fell to their drinking and dancing, even before the music began in earnest.

"I know not what to say!" said the poor elderly gentleman.

"Just love me as much as you do your port, and care for me better than you do your feet, which I hear need much attention, and all shall be well. Our dancing and future marriage shall be the stuff of legend!"

I feel bad now as I write this account and think of his confused face, but it is good to make my court laugh. They always love me the more for it.

18th February

Today I turned ten years old. I feel so much more grown up. Nine is a childish age, and now being ten, I can really bloom. I long to be taller. Father is tall, so I hope to be as well. I have had glorious presents from him and Mother, and so many packages arrived yesterday and today that the servants could speak of nothing else.

"How beloved you are, Your Highness!" exclaimed Lizzie Pole, handing me a box covered in organza ribbons. For once I nodded and smiled. She is right. Maybe not by everyone, but by everyone who really matters. The box was full of candied nuts – sent from Verona no less! I will savour every single one.

I have new dresses and shoes, all the latest fashions from London, each cut a little big for me in the hope that I will grow more, I imagine. There are velvets and silks, and an ermine edged muff which Mother says is to keep my hands warm when out walking, even though the winter is almost over.

We had a party with all kinds of sweetmeats laid out and a delicious plum cake. Prior More had thought of everything and spared no expense. Wolsey sent me a new batch of quills made from swan feathers, along with the very best ink. I hope he has no idea of my diary writing.

The ladies had prepared me a set of songs which they sang very prettily. And the feast this evening was my favourite – honeyed venison with red wine. Yes, I have celebrated in style today and am rather full and proud of myself as I write this account before bed.

10th March

I am rather glum today and find myself writing in my diary before anyone else is up. My erstwhile fiancé, Charles, the Holy Roman Emperor, marries that upstart Isabella this afternoon. I cannot help but feel put out and cast aside. He was promised to me, and I to him, for the longest time, and I had quite set my heart on being called an Empress.

But battles, subterfuges and financial negotiations have all conspired to return me to a princess – for now. I am quite sure I shall be queen one day. Whether just of England or by a good marriage, of France and elsewhere too, I do not know. To be destined Empress one month and then to be fighting one's own half-brother to even stay heiress of England's throne the next is galling to say the least.

2nd April

Soon the next stage of our journey begins, and I must say goodbye to Worcester and to my new friend, Prior More. We are moving on to Hartlebury next week, and then if the plague behaves its rotten self, to Ludlow at last. What's more, it has been raining almost non-stop. This has meant little or no riding and very few walks. I am supposed to get lots of fresh air but not when it is wet. Lady Margaret and my mother are always so anxious about my getting ill. They have lost too many dear ones to agues and sicknesses, I suppose. It is nice to be so loved but infuriating to be coddled sometimes.

This afternoon I buried my head in Latin exercises and

had a nice daydream about how I shall spend my days when I am queen. There will be no teachers or professors or lady governesses to rule my days then! I shall eat sweetmeats all day and go riding, and entertain dignitaries at court with my wonderful music, and all of Europe shall regard me the greatest musician in the world and bring me presents. I won't have to marry anyone and can sing and dance and eat plum cake whenever I like!

"What is the correct past participle, here, Mary? Princess Mary?" The drone of Dr Fetherstone's voice broke into my reverie.

Ugh. Latin is so utterly dull. And Latin teachers doubly so.

4th May

We have finally arrived at Ludlow!

The battlements on the outer bailey are huge! Just the sort of battlements a dragon would perch upon! My father was told by a Spanish ambassador once of a real dragon's footprint found from ages past, baked hard by the sun into stone. He said it was six spans of a man's hand across and had talons the size of daggers. I remember because I was hiding behind the throne at the time and the thought of it made me shudder.

By the time we'd driven through the gates, waving to all the well-wishers, then dismounted, the light was already beginning to fail, and I knew that a proper tour would not happen until the morrow. I could see there would be a lot to explore. There was a round tower in the middle of the inner bailey which looked intriguing, and of course tall ones on the corners of the outer bailey. This was a proper castle, and here I was to be a proper princess. I rushed eating my jugged hare and could not wait for the next day to dawn. What wonders it might reveal! Tomorrow night we will dine in the Great Hall, and there will be lots of important guests. It is going to be hard to sleep tonight and not just because it is yet another new bed!

5th May

I woke with the dawn even though the curtains were thick tapestry. It was so early that I saw the maid lighting my fire. I did not stir straight away in case I put her off her work. To be truthful, the chamber, though impressively large, was fairly warm already, it being May. When she'd finished, I asked her to draw the curtain back a little. Lady Catherine says I mustn't do this in case anyone sees me in my nightgown, but I shall stay well back. In any case, I was almost knocked backwards by the strength of the sunlight! Even at this early hour, the light streamed in.

Looking out with my hand over my eyes, I could see that we faced the round tower which Lady Margaret had already told me was the chapel. It is a very quick distance indeed from my chamber, although down a staircase. I shall be keen to see the inside of a round chapel! I pulled the cord to summon my ladies.

Once dressed, I was keen to see the Great Hall. We had come into this solar tower a different way yesterday, and I could see there was another staircase. Joy of joys, a spiral one! I love a spiral staircase, and such a grand one too! I like to stand on tiptoe and see how fast I can run up or down the narrowest ledge at its centre. Mrs. Pole, another of my ladies in waiting, says I might fall and break my neck, but then grown-ups are always saying such things.

"Who will rule England then, Your Highness?!" she said once.

"What a dull question," I replied. "Whoever is next in line, of course!"

Honestly, I do think Mrs. Pole rather tiresome. And Lizzie, her daughter, is sometimes just as bad. I wonder sometimes at them being part of Lady Margaret's family.

The staircase was great fun, even though in my haste to explore I may have ruined my silken slippers. No matter. I will get Ferrers to order more. The Great Hall is much larger than any I've seen so far, with very fine oak panels. I shall enjoy presiding over meals here. And the throne is much more luxurious than the chairs that have passed as one until now! It is lined with red velvet and is gilded with real gold. I ran out to look about the inner bailey and almost collided with Lady Catherine.

"Princess Mary, really!" she said.

"Yes?" I replied.

She frowned.

"Your Highness knows perfectly well that you should not be seen running! A princess does not run!"

I stuck my chin in the air.

"Why not?"

No-one has ever answered this question properly.

"Because it is undignified! A princess must glide, like so," she demonstrated. With her satin skirts skimming the ground, she really did look like she was on wheels.

"It makes you look like a ghost," I said, and wrinkled my nose at her.

I'm still not sure whether I entirely trust Lady Catherine, though clearly my father does, else she would not be part of my royal household.

"Also, what if I need to get somewhere fast? What if my people need me urgently?"

"Your people will always wait for you."

I put my head on one side to think about this. I suppose it is true.

"Indeed, Your Highness, sometimes it is good for them if you make them wait. It reminds them who is in charge."

"I suppose. I am going to see the chapel, will you come? A princess should never go anywhere unaccompanied."

She smiled and almost laughed.

"Of course, Your Highness."

The chapel was so strange, so round, and yet the altar was set to the east as it should be. But with no chancel, it seemed odd. The ceiling was very high, and there were many windows, filling the place with light. There was a tapestry of a woman in a garden, which I liked. The background was worked in a pale blue with a little gold, so that it looked like dawn, and I realised that the big stone thing in the background was the empty tomb.

"Mary Magdalene?" I guessed.

My companion nodded.

"This chapel is dedicated to her."

"So, I am Mary in Mary's chapel."

"Indeed."

"There you are, Highness!"

Countess Margaret had come to find me. She did not much like me to be out of her sight. She bowed to Lady Catherine who returned the greeting.

"I must be seeing to my husband's business," said Lady

Catherine. "I'm sure the Lady Margaret is keen to show you around, Princess."

"You may go," I said.

I went outside with Lady Margaret. We climbed up to the battlements of the outer bailey and looked out over the River Teme. It was sparkling in the spring sunshine. You could see the trout circling in the water even from up here. We looked across to the towers. Lady Margaret was giving me a history lesson, none of which I can remember now, about who built what and which noble added which improvements.

One thing that I do remember was the story about how those in the castle loyal to Queen Matilda were overthrown by a traitor who wanted her cousin Stephen as king. I wondered if I would be like Matilda and be ousted by a man with less claim to the throne. I'm thinking of Richmond of course. He may only be a half-brother, but being male seems to be more important – to barons four hundred years ago as well as to lords now!

I was lost in annoyance about this injustice for a moment. But then something so strange happened, it gave me odd chills. I will have to write about it tomorrow as my candle is almost down to the stump.

6th May

Now I have gathered myself, I can write of what happened yesterday. Lady Margaret and I were standing on the battlements looking down at the river; as I turned around I caught a glimpse of a woman by the Pendover Tower and wondered who she was.

"And you say no-one lives here at present?"

"No, Madam. As you know, this is one of your father's estates. Before your retinue arrived, there were only the steward and the servants here. Oh, and the tradesmen doing the repairs of course."

"Then who, pray, is that?"

I pointed at the woman in white at the foot of the tower.

The Countess peered intently.

"I see no-one, Your Highness."

"There, for goodness' sake, Lady Margaret, right there. A woman in bright white is walking around and around wailing. Can you not hear her? Is she too far away for you to see?"

"Mary," she replied, and I knew she was cross, because Lady Margaret only ever called me Mary when she was vexed, "Mary, there is nothing wrong with my eyesight. And I do not appreciate having tricks played on me. Quite plainly there is no-one there at all."

"I'm not playing tricks. Lady Margaret, truly from my heart, I am not! She is right there!"

"Well, I'm sorry Mary, I see and hear no-one. Now I must go and see that your chamber is ready."

She nodded to Mrs. Pole. "Constance, you stay with the Princess." Constance merely curtsied.

Now I was more intrigued by the figure, but also annoyed that Lady Margaret was cross with me. I peered at the figure and began to walk towards her, though the incline was something fierce.

"You see her, don't you, Mrs. Pole?" I said, but she just shook her head and then looked at her feet. Then when I looked back at the tower, the woman was gone. Well, I was quite sure I didn't imagine her. Perhaps she ran off into the woods. I will try to find out who she was. Someone here must know.

7th May

Bad news this morning. The rooms are not as ready as we might have liked, and we shall have to decamp yet again. Lady Catherine stayed last night and got rained on through the ceiling of her room, apparently.

"It's not funny, Mary, that could have been you!" Lady Margaret seemed only half-hearted in her admonishment as I giggled.

I do not think there is much love lost between her and Lady Catherine. They both think themselves in charge of me, no doubt. Well, I'm in charge of myself – and them – thank you very much. Lady Margaret looked out of the casement at the rain and her face looked worn, a little wan and tired. Though my mind was full of it, I decided not to ask about the White Lady again just yet. My governess was clearly preoccupied with other things. I would get Hazel to see if the other servants know who the mysterious stranger is instead.

"Lady Margaret?" she turned to me.

"Yes, Your Highness?"

"You don't like it here, do you?" I ventured. "This castle, I mean. Something about it upsets you."

"You are very astute sometimes, which is good. That will serve you well. It is good for a ruler to know what other people are thinking."

"Yes. But you did not answer my question."

She smiled.

"And to know when they are evading you."

She sighed and gazed back out of the window. "I stayed here once before, with your mother and your uncle. They were just married and happy."

"My mother… was married before?" I was astonished.

"Oh Mary, I'm sorry. I forgot myself. I thought you knew of it. Well, since I have begun… Yes, your mother was first married to your father's brother, Arthur. They came here for their honeymoon. I was in charge of your mother's household at that time. Then, they both got very sick."

"With the plague?"

"No. Something else. The apothecary said it was the sweating sickness. They call it ague sometimes. It can be deadly."

I couldn't believe what I was hearing. Why had I not been told about this?! I knew of Arthur, my father's older brother, but had no idea he was married to Mother or what became of him. I can imagine why Father kept this from me. The shame has silenced him. But Mother?

"And my mother clearly survived, but Arthur…"

"No, Arthur did not make it."

Lady Margaret burst into tears. I was shocked. She so rarely showed emotion. "That poor, dear boy, who should have been King!" She coloured and put a kerchief to her eyes to dry them.

"Instead, my mother was then married to my father?"

"Yes. Mere months later. But I have said too much, Mary. Please, don't ask me more. I care for your mother very greatly, as you know, as indeed I do for you, and it was a sad time as I had to nurse them both. Bad memories is all. Now, time to practise your spinet before dinner. Best

74

do so before it gets packed up again."

I had forgotten we would be moving on again.

"Where shall we be going now?" I asked, with a groan. "I am so tired of not knowing where I am when I wake."

"We shall be here a few days whilst arrangements are made. And these chambers will remain yours as we will return from time to time, Your Highness. It is the seat of power here for your father, so you must be seen here. But I believe Lord Dudley has found us a place nearby, at St Peter's Abbey, and then perhaps back to Tewkesbury Manor, which I know you liked. It does have immaculate gardens. More like home."

Like Ditton I suppose she meant, though right now, I can't remember what home feels like.

"We were seen to make such a grand entrance that we must stay here at least a fortnight," I pronounced, "otherwise people will think me weak and changeable. I will not have that. In fact, Lady Margaret, I wish it ordered that we shall split our time between here and Tewkesbury as necessary. It has taken us so long to get here, I want to be here as often as possible. Never mind the rotten builders."

"I will speak to Lord Dudley, Your Highness."

I nodded.

I do rather like the idea of Lady Catherine getting rained on just a little more.

10th May

Hazel told me at lunch that she found out the White Lady might be a ghost! They say one wails in white by the

Pendover Tower sometimes, which is where I saw her, and that she is a murderer! How exciting! I definitely don't want to leave Ludlow now!

There was a strange chill about the room as I climbed into bed tonight. Like that fresh wind in winter that sometimes takes you by surprise as you are riding, and places icy hands on your back, no matter how thick the clothing. I felt my very bones rattle. At first, I thought it was my imagination. But then I felt frosty breath on my neck.

"Who is there?" I called out. "Who is it? Who dares to touch the Princess?"

The silence after my outburst was as cold as the air. My own breath was cracking into frosted spikes before my eyes. At first I could not move, but then I felt strangely drawn to the window. This high up, there was little enough to see. Except… except there was that white shape drifting again, right at the foot of the tower. I shivered and determined to ask Ferrers about it in the morning.

And then I realised that the drifting shape was a reflection in the glass, and not outside at all. Whatever it was, it was now standing right beside me.

"If you are a ghost or spirit, some kind of phantom, you should know that I am a devout girl and I follow my Bible. It tells us not to speak with the dead."

I sounded braver than I felt.

And then it spoke, with a voice like icicles, sharp and frozen.

"Ah, Madam, but might you listen? How indeed could you not?"

"I might stop up my ears."

"You could try."

There was a harsh, frosty laugh.

"But in any case, I am not the dead speaking. I am only an echo."

"An echo?"

The spirit was barely visible, just a wisp of white and silver, catching here and there at the corners of my vision as she wafted about the chamber.

"When someone dies in great anguish, as I did, they leave behind an echo, a memory, an etching on the universe."

There was a pause as I thought about this.

"Like the way the hens still run around once their heads are chopped off?"

"Not the nicest example, but yes, something like that. So, I am Marjorie's pain. I scream out her pain of betrayal, the guilt of the murder she then committed, and the fall from this very tower that killed her."

Now this sounded interesting! My heart was racing.

"Tell me what happened?"

"Alas, alas Madam! I thought myself in love and loved in return. My lover would come and see me in that very tower. All in secret. So romantic!"

"Pah! Courtly love, no doubt! How did he get in?"

I should have been amazed that I was talking to a ghost, but I was more amazed by what we spoke of.

"I let down a ladder for him."

"Was it made of your own hair?"

"No. How would that happen? No-one has that much hair. Are you quite well? What a strange question."

This ghost had clearly not been read fairy tales.

"Never mind. Go on. He used to climb up here and woo you?"

"Yes, but it was all in secret because he was one of our enemies. His loyalties lay with Stephen and mine with Queen Matilda."

"You were letting an enemy into the castle? Regularly? And in the dark?"

I was pretty sure I could see where this was going. Marion obviously hadn't been the sharpest sword in the armoury.

"I sense you scoff at me, young madam. But you are too little yet to know the power that love can hold over a heart and indeed over a mind."

"Love seems to cause nothing but trouble."

"You will find out for yourself, no doubt."

"And then, what happened then?"

"I am... it is hard to speak of it. Even after all these centuries."

There was a small pause. Frost started to form on my looking glass next to the bed, and the water in my ewer began to freeze over.

"Perhaps because of all the centuries. If we linger on our pain, it grows."

"I suppose it well might. But have you come here to tell me your sad tale, or Marion's anyway. I would hear it."

"Yes. I have told you part. I may as well tell the rest. One night he was careful to leave the ladder down. I did not notice, for we were otherwise engaged. I...I believed he loved me."

Sobbing delayed her story telling. I had no sympathy. Only eagerness to hear more.

"A small group of soldiers climbed up, ready to storm the castle from the inside. I realised too late that my love had betrayed me. I had handed the enemy the victory. I was mortified and so very angry. My heart broke in two and I thought my head would split with the pain. I grabbed his own sword from the scabbard and slit his throat."

"Good," I said, which maybe wasn't all that kind, but it was what I thought. In my head I was imagining what that would look like, how much blood there might be.

"Good, you say, Madam? Good, aye the right thing to do but what had my foolishness cost? Already I could hear the screams of the others being put to death in their beds. I knew I could not live with myself, nor without my love. I ran to the tower window and threw myself down."

I sensed the ghost, or the echo, if you like, move back towards the casement, as though she was looking out.

"Down there, I fell, Madam, and it was a horribly long way."

If a ghost might shiver, I think she did then.

"And that was the end of Marion de la Bruges. Fool, and unwitting traitor."

More soft, cold sobbing in the dark. I gave her a moment and thought on her lament.

"Well, Marion, I am sorry for your tragic death. But I'm glad you got the devil before you leapt. He deserved it."

There was a long silence.

"In any case, I wonder if we might be of use to one another. We are both, perhaps, the victims of men who deceive us."

"I would help you, good young madam, if I can. I believe that the more good I do here, the more this echo would fade, and I might sigh away into nothing and be at peace. For now, adieu."

She faded away into nothing, just a few ice crystals hanging in the air.

As I write this down my hands are still shaking. I cannot believe I have spoken with a ghost! And one with such a sorry tale to tell! Not only is she a ghost, but she is *my* ghost; she came to me, and she might be my secret weapon in overcoming those who seek to defeat me.

17th May

Today I woke to an iron chill in the air. This has happened a few more times and I am getting used to it. I did not even flinch. I let myself come round then said, without opening my eyes,

"Good morrow, Marion."

"Good morrow, Princess. About time you woke up. It's almost nine of the clock!"

"Oh well, when you're a princess you can wake when you like," I thought about this, "sometimes."

I yawned and sat up, watching Marion floating around the room in her weightless fashion, her white dress sparkling like snow caught in first light.

"Very interesting, your plan to seek revenge on the lords," she said.

"My what?" my heart thumped hard in my chest. "Have you been listening at the door?"

"Ha! Of course not! I wouldn't stoop so low. I just read it in your book there."

A part of her, probably an arm, wafted grey mist in the direction of my journal. I sat up quickly, horrified, had I left it unlocked? Who else had seen it? I grabbed the book and held it to my chest defiantly.

"Dear me, such histrionics over the childish drivel

you've written."

I felt myself colour.

"And the feeble attempt at a code!"

"And you," I countered, "won't listen at a door but you're quite happy to read someone's private diary!"

If a ghost could grin, I swear Marion did.

"Oh well…. I was intrigued."

The lock was unbroken.

"Locks are no barrier to me, dear little Princess!" said Marion, watching where my eyes had lingered. "I can walk through walls! Anyway, your secrets are safe with me. We ARE friends, after all."

I wondered about this. Was I really friends with a ghost? It seemed unreal. I wondered if I should tell someone, like Lord Dudley, or Professor Duwes or even Lady Catherine. But they would just give me one of those disbelieving grown-ups looks, or worse, think me an utter fool. I can't bear to be thought stupid. I shook my head clear. Maybe, after all, Marion might be of more use than I'd ever imagined.

"Marion," I said, slowly and calmly, as I thought it through, "how would you feel about being my spy?"

"A spy?" she thought a minute, her soft grey shape slowly bobbing up and down in the sunlight. "That sounds exciting."

"It could be," I answered, with all the coolness I could muster. "If it were done well, by the right person. Someone clever, who understands plots and schemes."

"And who can waft through walls and read other people's diaries?"

I laughed.

"That too."

19th May

The door to the Great Hall burst open. Matthew ran up to me, his face pale and angry.

"Please, Your Highness, please come."

I went with him, telling Ferrers to continue without me. There were only a few trifling matters to deal with today anyway. I cannot be sure, but I think I saw Puce grin and nod at one of his lackeys.

Matthew waited for me and Lady Margaret to catch up and we walked quickly to the stables. God confound this idiocy that girls and women may not run!

Matthew waited until we were in the stables before shutting the door behind us.

"Princess Mary," he said, breathlessly, "Sheba…she has been poisoned."

"Is she okay?"

I looked round frantically. The dear little mare was asleep on the hay in her stall.

"She is fine. But someone mixed ragwort in with her oats. I am very careful, Your Highness, and I saw them before she had even one mouthful."

There was no point asking if it were a mistake or an accident. Everyone knew the bright yellow flower was poisonous to horses.

"Thank God you noticed, Matthew. Thank you!"

I went over to Sheba and patted her neck.

"I…I thought you should know straight away. And that whoever it was should be found and punished."

"Of course! Do you have any idea who it was?"

He shook his head.

"Did you see anyone skulking around the stables?"

"No, Your Highness. Sorry."

He hung his head.

"Matthew, you have served me well today, as you always do. I want you to remain watchful.

"Yes, Princess."

Tonight, as I write these words in my diary, I hope the guard I posted outside the stables will keep Sheba safe. But who would have tried to kill her? It can only have been someone intent on causing me distress. Would Gravenor and Puce, in league with Richmond, stoop so low?

Back in my chambers before my ladies came to dress me for dinner, Marion appeared, along with her customary chill. I shivered.

"What is it, Marion? Have you learned something?"

"Good evening, Your Highness. Your horse is quite well?"

"Yes, thank you. Matthew the groom was watchful. Why, do you know something about it?"

There was a pause.

"I saw two girls picking flowers out in the meadow today," she said. "One was that Clara."

She made a face. I had told her about Clara. Treachery and double-dealing did not sit well with Marion for obvious reasons.

"I did not recognize the other," she continued. "But they were laughing and joking, and when they came back to the house Clara went to the stables. I thought nothing of it at the time, else I should have warned you."

I scowled. That girl was cold and wicked.

"No, of course, Marion. How could you know such a cold heart beat in the breast of a small girl? Thank you, you have confirmed what I already suspected."

"I did love horses, my lady. When I was alive."

"I thought you were just an echo?"

The room grew colder, as it always did when Marion was sulking. Small icicles began to appear on the nightstand.

"Well, even echoes have memories. And feelings."

"I'm sorry. I did not mean to belittle your heart. You are a kind soul, Marion. Thank you for your service."

The room warmed.

"The ladies are coming," she said, and then disappeared.

At dinner, Lord Craddock (who is most fond of horses) inquired after Sheba's health.

"My horse is recovering well, thank you," I replied.

When Lord Gravenor spoke, he only confirmed my suspicions: "Forgive me, Your Highness, that tiny little thing is hardly a horse! We have moorland ponies taller than her across the border."

If he thought anyone would dare laugh with him, he was wrong.

"She may be small, but she has qualities some lack. She has courage and integrity and loyalty, to name but three."

He had the grace to colour a little at that.

"I value her as part of my court more than I do some people."

I could not help but look at Clara then, standing with Puce, pouring yet more of my wine into his goblet. She was looking at the floor. I wonder what other evils she might be capable of, and what those two Lords have promised her, or have over her, to make her act against me. I must be more on my guard. Next time it might be me they poison.

1st June

With the lords pulling against me, I thought I would try to find out more about their plans. Clara is pretending to eavesdrop on them, but of course, I have to discount all she says, since I know where her loyalties lie. Puce likes his ale, so perhaps he might let slip some information in the Great Hall at dinner. I decided to swap places with Hazel again and serve the gentlemen, keeping my ears open.

"Why don't you just let me keep my ears open, Your Highness?" Hazel asked calmly, "Rather than put our arrangement at risk?"

I laughed.

"Oh, I'm sure it will be fine. It will be rather fun to see how the men are when they are less on their guard."

Hazel bit her lip and looked doubtful. But I am the princess here, so we went ahead and changed clothes before dinner.

Portly Puce took another slug of ale from his tankard. His beard was dripping with it, and here and there, bits of meat and bone were tangled. Disgusting. I rarely got this close to him, thankfully. I could even smell the stench of stale ale. Before I even knew what was happening, he'd put his arm round me and pulled me towards his knee.

"Ha ha, little wench, what are you doing, looking so slyly at a gentleman like me? Maybe one day you'll be serving me in my house? What do you think? A rich, handsome man to wait on? You'd like that, wouldn't you?"

He laughed. I tried to pull free. As much as anything, I wanted to put my hand over my mouth to block his awful odour. The lords either side of him guffawed. Gravenor yawned and frowned a little.

"She's a child, Puce," he said. "Leave her be."

"You're right," said my enemy, looking straight at me but not seeing me at all. "No real meat on her yet!"

Some men see females as shapes, I think, not even as people. Still, I was worried he might recognise me, and my heart was pounding like a battle drum. He laughed again, but still held my wrist tightly so I could not get up. His grip was starting to burn.

"Let me go," I said quietly. He pretended not to hear.

"PUT THAT GIRL DOWN!" yelled a female voice, which he did listen to.

As far as Puce was concerned, Princess Mary was pointing straight at him. He had the wits to release me and the grace to blush a little.

"My servants are here to pour ale, not humour old men!" Hazel continued.

Everybody laughed but me. I felt a fool, and walked back out of the hall, through the kitchens and up to my apartments, rubbing my sore arm. A fine spy I was! I'd learned nothing about Puce except what I already suspected, that for all his pretence to nobility, he was a foul and filthy man with no morals. From now, on I will set others with more experience to the task. To think, our disguise might have been uncovered! Hazel has again proved her worth, and our ruse is working better than I could have thought. Perhaps it is time to make better use of Marion.

7th June

I have been thinking a lot, since Clara tried to give Sheba

ragwort, of poisons and how they work. Something about them has been nagging at the back of my mind.

"Marion," I asked, as she wafted in the soft light of morning, "what do you know of poisons?"

She flew up to me, very excitedly.

"Poisons, Your Highness? Are you wanting to kill someone? To watch them die in horrible agony?"

"Err no," I said, surprised by her keenness. "And I thought we decided you had a good heart?"

"It depends on who the victim is," she said, and I swore I could see her teeth baring. "Some people deserve to die. There was a prince here, once, got poisoned. Not long ago," she said, as if drifting in her thoughts as well as through the chamber.

I sat up straight.

"Not long ago? But before I was born?"

"Yes, here in this very castle. He was Prince of Wales, just as you are Princess of Wales. Heir to the throne."

"Here with his young bride?"

My voice trembled to think the ghost was talking about my uncle.

"Yes, that's it. A relative of yours I think?"

I nodded.

"How was he poisoned, Marion? I thought he had the sweating sickness?"

"Oh, the cure caused that. No, it was another of these wretched spies…" she wafted her hand in the air, as though it were full of them. "Deadly nightshade. In his food."

But this was terrible! Someone had killed my uncle? But who? Who stood to gain? And the answer of course, made my blood run cold. My father. My father who then married the young prince's widow and became king hereafter. Surely this could not be true?

"But Marion, what do you mean when you say the cure killed him?"

"Ask the old man. The apothecary. He will tell you."

And with that, most unlike her usual self, as though she were bored of the whole conversation, she faded away without so much as a by your leave. I was left in anguish. I must visit this old man she spoke of and discover the truth. Sleep may be hard to find tonight.

8th June

I am desperate to meet the apothecary and know his truths. Meeting him won't be easy and comes with huge risks, so I will have to bide my time and hope the opportunity arises. I asked Hazel if she knew of him.

"Oh yes, Your Highness. He is a strange, wizened man. They say he's travelled all over the world and that he has special potions that stop you from dying and that's why he has lived to such a ripe old age." She wrinkled her nose a bit, "He looks like a pickled walnut."

I laughed. I liked Hazel. So much so that I had warned her more clearly than the others about speaking freely around Clara, although I hadn't told her why. I asked where the man lived, and she told me. I will make plans to meet him.

The weather is very fine, so I am being let off more and more lessons to ride and get fresh air. Lady Margaret has been worried for my health. Perhaps she is finally listening to my complaints that Latin makes me ill. At least we have the players to look forward to next week.

12th June

"Mister Shakespeare," I asked, as soon as I could after another wonderful performance, this time of a play about the Fates, "your scripts are of the highest quality. They must be written by someone most learned." I paused. "Presumably not you."

He feigned hurt.

"Your Highness! Do you not think me learned? Why I know my A, B, C and almost all the other letters!"

I laughed.

"The plays, the good ones, that you discern, Your Highness, not the pageants, are written by someone dear to me. But I have promised never to tell who."

"I see. And would this person take commissions at all? Royal commissions?"

He flushed with pride.

"I believe she, I mean…he would."

He winced. It was a woman! I was astonished. Not that a woman could write so well, I believe us quite the equal of men in most things bar jousting, but that she had managed to gain such an education.

"That's good news," I said. "I have some work for this person which I need completed before Christmas. On another matter entirely," I said, winking at him (at least I think I was winking, for it isn't something I'm practiced at), "shall I ever have the honour of meeting your wife?"

"I think that my Abigail would like that very much, Your Highness. but currently, she is in her confinement. We should be parents very soon!"

"Then for goodness' sake go to her, Mister Shakespeare. She shall have need of you!"

"I doubt it, good madam," said the rascal. "Birth and babies are matters for the women. I should only be in the way."

He had a point. Fathers seemed to take all the credit for a healthy newborn, but the risk was very much the mother's. I had seen the devastation of this up close with my own mother. She never spoke of her other children, all of whom have died except me.

I wonder why I was spared. I wonder if God wants me to be queen. But then, why should my brother, little Prince Edward, have died at just a few months old? He surely had done no wrong. This all went through my mind as Mister Shakespeare rattled on about his wife and his hopes for a son. Daughters, of course, never seem very important, unless they are all you have.

"Well, I should like to meet your child, and more importantly, your wife, when they are able to make the journey."

"Oh, well now, that's a grand royal invitation, thank you, Your Highness. I shall bring them as soon as they can manage the cart. I know you'll love my Abigail. She has ideas about women being as good as men, much like yourself." I smiled.

And, if I were right, and it were Abigail who wrote the scripts for the plays, she must be a clever woman, and perhaps well-read. Yes, I thought I would very much like to meet her.

15th June

It has been a long time since the feast when I swapped

places with Hazel, but I have been itching to play a trick on the grotty Puce ever since. Today we were to have a special dinner for some of the local lords, and it seemed a good time to get my revenge.

As I was dressing for the meal, Hazel was pilfering some pigs' eyeballs from the kitchens at my command. She was to put them in a leather pouch at her waist and hold onto them until just the right moment. She popped her head round the corner of my chambers just as I was about to descend, and grinned, holding the offending bag by its drawstrings and waving them at me.

"Want to see them?" she laughed.

I made a face.

"No, thank you! You know what to do with them. Await my signal."

The other ladies looked bemused.

"You are not up to any mischief are you, Your Highness?" asked Lady Catherine, who had come to inspect my final appearance.

I rolled my eyeballs.

"Princesses are not mischievous, Lady Catherine. You of all people should know that."

Cecily and Ann snorted. They love it when I'm cheeky and get away with it. I'm sure my ladies-in-waiting think as I do – they just can't get away with acting as I do.

The lords bowed as I entered the Great Hall to take my place at the head of the banquet. Some lower than others, I noticed. I keep my eyes out for such signs. Those who bow very low are either rightfully respectful or wanting to seem it, and they are often after a favour. Those who barely nod are wondering why they are asked to defer to a young girl and don't like it and are people I need to be wary of. I am more inclined to trust those who bow or curtsey just enough, the men bending their backs, and the ladies bobbing for at least a few seconds. They are showing proper respect without overdoing it. Puce bows too low and Gravenor barely nods at all.

Dudley had written me a pretty speech, thanking these "gracious barons," for their help and hospitality to the crown. I was standing as I spoke, and waved my hand to one side, which was the signal to Hazel, before adding my own line,

"All of you are so brave and courageous, it is an honour to be amongst such lionhearts," I began, as Hazel opened the bag and put its contents into Puce's goblet. "A toast then, to courage!"

I raised my goblet, and took a sip of wine, waiting for the delicious moment of revenge to arrive. My anxious heart was beating fast. Wonderfully though, as glasses were lowered, Puce let out a girlish shriek, a squeal worthy of a pig at slaughter. He spat out his drink, throwing its ghastly contents everywhere and ran from the room.

"Yes," I continued, barely missing a beat, "Courage, which most of you have in abundance."

The room erupted in laughter. Through the windows, it being summer, there was enough light to see Puce outside, running around and vomiting everywhere. Hazel was bent double with laughter at the back of the room, and I must confess, I encouraged it in all those before me. Revenge tasted sweet – unlike Puce's wine.

30th July

There has not been much to write about lately, but today I met Abigail Shakespeare, along with her little boy. Ludlow is nearer the Shakespeares' farm than my previous residences, so it was not too taxing a journey, I hope.

The playwright was tall and slender, most pretty with dark hair and eyes, a little younger than her husband, who beamed with pride as she curtsied expertly, even whilst holding John. I enquired after their health, and she thanked me most profusely for the silver spoon and plate I had sent as a baptism gift. He was a sweet, handsome baby boy.

"He appears to have his father's appetite already," I said, "judging from that girth."

They all laughed. As the men gathered round to rehearse, I had the opportunity I was waiting for and outlined the play I wished to commission. Abigail nodded and handed the baby to her husband so that she might take some notes.

"You are very well-educated for a farmer's wife," I hazarded.

"Thank you, Your Highness. I learnt to read at a young age and never stopped."

I smiled.

"I find that most admirable, Mrs. Shakespeare. You please me and may come to court with young John whenever you find yourself able."

She curtsied again.

"I much appreciate the honour, Your Highness, and the confidence you have placed in my abilities."

"Your secret talent is safe with me, I might add," I said.

"I know how many men would react to words penned by a woman."

She sighed with relief.

"Thank you, Your Highness. Yes, it is much better that I remain anonymous. I must admit I was very anxious when Richard told me he had let it slip. But I have heard you are a good princess and practice your devotions. I am glad to see these things are true."

We bowed heads to one another, and I left the troupe to their business. Doubtless they will stay another week or so and entertain us well.

2nd August

My curiosity about the sweating sickness finally got the better of me today. I had Lady Margaret come with me to meet the apothecary. Abigail Shakespeare was standing by the castle gates with her young charge as we left. It was looking like rain as I bade them into the carriage.

"Is your husband nowhere to be found? Have you come in search of him?" I asked.

"Indeed, Your Highness. For a large man he can be surprisingly hard to locate, at times."

"We are off to visit an old apothecary, simply for his stories and to get out of the castle for a while. It might be a distraction. Should you like to accompany us? We will soon find that rogue husband of yours when we get back."

"Indeed, that would be most interesting, Your Highness, if you don't mind John. He is a good child, but I can't vouch for his quietness."

"No indeed, especially if he takes after his father."

We laughed and the carriage was ordered onwards.

The old doctor lived above his little shop and came down to greet us. Or rather, the guards brought him down. I do not travel anywhere without a little backup unless I am pretending to be Hazel. The ancient oak beams inside the shop were so warped and old that the place seemed as wizened as its proprietor. There were stacks of clay jars, even some made of glass, and so many muslin bags of mysterious roots and dried seed pods that one wondered how he could tell one from another. Everything was very carefully labelled but the old man's script was not clear, and often bleached by the sun.

He bowed and scraped as he showed us round, regaling us with tall stories, and speaking of poisons and their antidotes, as I'd hoped he would.

"No, Highness, do not touch that, I beg of you," the old man said, as I reached up for a jar with a few dried brown seeds in it. In faded hand the label read: "Carabar. Poison – deadly."

"Oh, why does it say that? I believed Carabar to be a cure for illness?" I exclaimed.

"Yes, for the poison dripped by Belladonna, for anything else, it would kill you just as surely. A slow, painful death of sweating and sickness."

That was interesting. As was the fact that Lady Margaret looked anxious.

"Much like the ague?"

"Far worse than that, Your Highness. Few recover. It is very powerful. Very rare too. Beyond price."

"Then how do you have any?"

"Oh. I came by these beans as a much younger man. I

travelled a great deal then and traded with merchants and apothecaries in the seaports. Even with the Moors and the Saracens. There were a great deal of exotic silks and spices to buy then, but I was always more interested in poisons and their cures."

"And have you ever had cause to use these terrible beans?"

The apothecary looked me in the eye then, and I could have sworn that right at that moment, his memory was as clear as his crystal blue eyes.

"Just once, Highness. Just once. A young man was poisoned, and possibly his bride too, though we gave her a much smaller dose."

"And she recovered, but he did not."

He shuffled uncomfortably from one Turkish-slippered foot to another.

"Aye, Highness. A sad business."

"I really think we should be going, now, Your Highness," interjected Lady Margaret. "It is only an hour from dinner, and you have yet to change."

"I will stay, if you please," I said firmly.

The discomfort on her face was telling me as much as the old man's words. As he turned to answer some question of Abigail's, I whispered to my other companion. "Did you know about this, Lady Margaret? Did you suspect?"

"I was afraid. So afraid that your father had something to do with it Your Highness. He was so angry when Katharine... when your mother came down with it too. Kept saying someone had been careless. I hoped it wasn't true."

Lady Margaret began to weep. She so rarely wept. I wasn't sure how to react. I pulled everything inside together, to one single aim. If this were true, as I'd suspected, then my father's reputation was at stake. Princes go round killing people of course, it is almost expected. Respected. But to kill your own brother to gain his wife and throne? That was the sort of thing that only happened in plays, wasn't it?

That reminded me, Abigail the playwright was listening to all this. Standing in the corner, after distracting the old man for me, she was now trying to pretend she wasn't there. Probably wishing she were anywhere else. I beckoned her over. The old man knew less than we did of the matter – despite being there at the time. I waited for him to move away, which did not take long. He was happier in the company of his jars and poultices than with three women and a small baby.

"What this elderly gentleman has told us today, what it might mean, what light it sheds on my father's character, never mind his claim to the throne… this stays between us three. Agreed?"

Margaret dabbed her eyes with her kerchief as she nodded. Her loyalty was guaranteed since she knew how the Tudor family dealt with loose tongues. Abigail nodded too, but she said nothing. What could I do to entreat her silence?

"Highness," she said whilst I was thinking. "I shall not speak or write of this, I promise you. Not as long as you or your father draw breath."

This was an odd promise, as though she might speak of it after my father's death – or mine. But her looks were true, and I could only thank her and be glad.

"But what of the old man, Mary?" asked Margaret, worriedly. "If he told us these things, what is to stop him speaking to others?"

I reached up and carefully took down the jar of seeds. I tucked them under my cape.

"None will believe him. I will have it spread about that he is old and unreliable. We will take care of him, but he must not be allowed to practice any longer."

In my head, I was wondering if this was good enough, whether more drastic action was needed. I knew what Father would do. The thought of it first chilled my bones...then rather excited me. The gory scene lingered before I shook it from my head. I would be merciful and let him live, unscathed. If the secret had stayed buried all this time, my father no doubt had seen it buried.

1st September

I am to see Mother and Father! We are packing even now, and they are headed to us likewise and we shall meet for a month as a floating court. I am so happy. I have been dancing around the room and singing ever since Mother's letter came. Lady Margaret has been admonishing me and saying I should show more decorum. I confess, I stuck my tongue out at her. Not very princess-like of me, but I can't be perfect all the time.

We shall meet them at the Old Palace of Langley, near Woodstock Palace. There will be lots of exploring to do, Mother says, since Father can't bear to be stuck indoors when away from London. We shall visit places together as a proper family. I will pack my diary away, as I do not intend to write much whilst we are together. I will write of it later.

2nd September

I asked Marion if she might accompany me to Langley, because I know I should miss her advice, but she said she cannot leave the environs of the castle.

"I am tied to it, Your Highness, like a tethered goat. The stones of the building are alive in my bones."

This sounded very odd, but I sort of knew what she meant. It made me sad, but of course there was nothing we could do about it.

I went out to the Magdalene chapel whilst my ladies were packing. There was a loose stone from the building work by the entrance which I kicked in frustration. Something made me look more closely at it. It was not a new stone brought in for repairs, but an old one, part of the chapel that had recently fallen. Not too large. I tried to lift it and found a corner of it that was cracked and broke off easily. I put that piece in my pocket.

I gave orders for the trip and left some for whilst I was away. Clara was not to come with me, and I told Dudley, who was also staying behind, to keep an eye on her and the wicked lords. He was most alarmed that I thought her a spy. I did not want to risk her doing anything to Sheba, so I thought I had better say. He seemed pleased that I trusted him, and cross at the same time, for keeping him in the dark for so long.

"How can I protect you, Princess Mary, if you do not trust me?"

I did feel bad. But one has to suspect everyone to reach the throne, I think.

Marion was most taken with the idea of travelling with a piece of the castle stone. I am going to put it in my trunk, and she will see if she can attach herself to it and come with me. It is an experiment for sure, but it shows I can be quite clever when I need to be, and when it has nothing to do with Latin.

10th September

Well, I had to dig my diary out, or rather, get Lady Margaret to do it (she thinks it contains extra Latin exercises). So much is wrong here that I need to write it down to help make sense of it.

At first everything was wonderful. Once out of the carriage I was given a warm reception. The servants all clapped, my mother ran to me and hugged me, and then my father lifted me high in the air whilst declaring how much I had grown.

There was to be a feast in the hall to celebrate this new roaming court. Lots of guards were posted with halberds at all the entrances. They looked very grand in their uniforms. Up in my new chambers, there were presents laid out, including a new dress made of blue velvet, and a matching headdress with an ivory band and three teardrop pearls sewn into it. Hazel was gasping at the beauty of it, and I grinned. She was wondering if she would get to wear it no doubt!

Mother came in to see how I liked her gift.

"Mija! What do you think? It suits your hair, no? You are starting to turn red like your father."

"I love it, Mother!" we hugged.

I was loath to let go. Unusually for her, she began to sob.

"Is something wrong?" I asked at last. She pulled back

and wiped her eyes.

"No, my dear one." She smiled her brave smile. "All is well. I am just emotional to see you. It has been a long time and your father…" the sentence tailed off.

What was she going to say? Had he stopped her coming to see me? She had not been writing so often either. Had I done something wrong? But these were not questions I could ask.

There was much cheering as we went down to the feast. The ale and wine always flowed generously and began early in the day at the English court. However, there was something amiss. The room may have been warm, but there was a coldness between my parents. They had always been so happy. At least, I thought so.

This felt different. I sensed an anger, a confusion in my father that was hard to place. He no longer sat near my mother, or showed her any affection, and she no longer looked at him. There was much drinking, much feasting, but no laughter.

11th September

Father is quite proud of Ampthill Castle, it being a new acquisition. Mother found it cold and kept shivering despite being well wrapped in her furs and the day being bright. The housekeeper showed us around with Mother saying very little as Father waxed lyrical about the greatness of the rooms. Eventually what little patience he had was exhausted.

"Honestly, woman, you are never happy anywhere!

Another time I might send you here to wallow in your own misery!"

Father stormed off to look at the upper apartments by himself, leaving Mother in tears, and myself and the housekeeper quite bewildered.

"He likely *will* send me here!" Mother wailed. "I am of no use to him now! And yet I shall pray for strength, Mary. Will you join me?"

We headed back to the chapel, and I had little choice but to kneel next to Mother on the flagstone floor and pray the rosary. Mother spent the whole time gazing at the altar, tears constantly flowing. I did not know what was wrong or what I was supposed to do. My knees were sore, so I put a hassock under them. This was hardly the family reunion I had longed for!

Later, as we gave up on Father and called for the carriage, I saw him outside by the gates, gazing at something in his hand. As we drove off, he closed it, and I realised it was a locket. I doubted it was a picture of me or of his wife he was looking at so adoringly. Perhaps it was a miniature of my so-called brother. He may not be here with us, but I feel the wedge of him between us all the same.

13th September

"Good morrow, Mistress Mary!" the familiar chill dusted the room with icy crystals.

"Marion! Where've you been? I've been wanting to speak with you!"

I yawned and sat up, rubbing the sleep from my eyes.

The pale light told me it was just before dawn.

"Ah! All this moving about. It is hard to keep track of myself. Being tied to the stone is not as easy as I thought it might be. The further I am from the Pendover Tower, the less myself I feel."

"I am sorry. We will get you back there very soon. Does it feel odd?"

"Yes," she tried to think. "Like I am sand in an hourglass with eight different bulbs."

I was not awake enough to figure out what she meant.

"How goes your family holiday?" she asked. "I have been watching you when I can. It does not seem all that happy."

"It is not, Marion. Mother cries and Father shouts and neither of them seem to take much notice of me."

"I am sorry. It must be painful."

"Yes."

"But you wanted to speak with me? Was there something in particular?"

Her silver shape drifted around the room, shimmering as the first rays of sun came through the casement.

"Well, I did want to see a friend. I have been lonely. Only a few of my ladies have come and they are mostly needed elsewhere."

"I have seen Lady Margaret hiding in your chambers in the day."

"Does she? I think she is frightened of Father."

If ghosts shrugged, that's what Marion did.

"Most people are, I imagine. With good reason."

"Perhaps there is another darling," Marion mumbled.

"What makes you say that?"

I was eager to know what she had seen.

"Ah, well. When married people argue, there usually is."

I gulped: "Father has had affairs before. Kings do."

"I feel this is different. More serious," Marion explained.

"Why?"

"He has a picture of her in a locket."

I nodded and asked, intrigued: "Did you get to see who it was?"

"I saw the picture. I got right up close to his shoulder and gave him the shivers. But then the stone pulled me back."

"So, who was it?"

"Highness, how should I know? Some pretty young woman. I do not know your court."

Of course Marion wouldn't know who it was. How could she?

Then she added, "But I could show you."

"Show me, how?"

"What use is a spy if she cannot remember things?"

On the looking glass in front of us, a layer of frost began to form, and then in it, a portrait started to appear. Marion was drawing the woman in the locket!

"How clever you are, Marion!"

The face and hair started to become real. I was transfixed. When her work was complete, a face sparkled in the dawn light. There before me, was a very good likeness of one of the court ladies. Prettier than when I last saw her but unmistakably Lady Anne Boleyn.

20th September

Today at luncheon we had a picnic in the grounds of the

lodge. It was sunny but not exactly warm. We were sheltered on one side by a brick wall. Father spoke of building an orangery there, since the sun pooled nicely in the corner. But the pleasantries did not last long.

"And so, Mary, dear daughter, we must get serious about having you married off. Suitors have been less forthcoming as you grow older. It is normally the other way round."

Was he trying to upset me? He certainly upset Mother, who concentrated hard on her bread and honey.

"I believe that is more to do with the changing fortunes of England, than the charms of her princess," I countered, lifting my chin so he could see I was not afraid of his teasing, if that's what it was.

He laughed, I think good-naturedly.

"Ah, Mary, I see you are learning to give as good as you get. No milksop you! Well, I am glad you have some fire in you. I know where you get that from!"

Did I have his fire? Maybe. But with people, my blood ran colder. I was beginning to care less what they thought. I would do my duty before God and country, but if my own parents didn't want to love me, I saw no point trying to get anyone else to. Yes, I was colder now than when I left London. One of my best friends was a ghost after all.

"You are thinking hard. Whom should you like to marry out of all the kings and princes of Europe?"

I shook my head at him.

"None of them will love me. I am a means to a throne, that's all."

"Ah, you want love, Mary? That will not do. Love does not last."

Mother bristled.

"Then why do people risk everything for it?" I countered.

He had the grace to blush a little at that. But I had got a little too close to his own thoughts and angered him. Talking to Father was like stroking a bull. If you got the wrong spot, he would bellow.

"Most are fools!" he snorted. "Anyway, Mary, your fate is now decided, whether you like it or not. You were to be betrothed to the Dauphin's younger brother, but we have now decided that Francis himself will be a better match, though I'll try to keep your options open. Hopefully, in the spring."

I was shocked. Francis was in his thirties. How could Father think him a good match for a girl of ten? I felt sick.

"And will he wait for me to be old enough? Shall he keep his promise? Unlike his son before him or the Emperor Charles?"

"Do men ever?" Mother spoke, finally, and her tone was full of something I'd not heard in her voice before.

Father ignored her. We carried on with our picnic as though my life hadn't just been mapped out and none of us raised the subject again. But perhaps this is good news? If Father is still wanting to marry me off, I must still be his official heir. Maybe Richmond is out of the picture after all?

A terrible thought occurred to me. If my half-brother did overtake me in the stakes for the English throne, he might, in time, succumb to the same sweating-sickness as my uncle. That could, after all, be arranged, given the small jar of death I was keeping safe. If a future King might kill with impunity, why not a future Queen?

2nd October

Goodbyes were painful, and it was especially hard to drag myself out of my mother's arms. She was in floods of tears and speaking of never seeing me again. I cried too and eventually Lady Margaret saw fit to gently part us.

"You will make yourself ill, Your Highness. Your mother's misery is not yours to bear."

Knowing how dear my mother was to her too, she must be hurting for us both. This whole month, which was meant to be joyful, has been a time of sorrow, seeing my parents so distant, Father so nasty to Mother, and so cool with me.

My court has been waiting for me at Tickenhill House near Worcester. My mother told me she has happy memories of the place, but I had to ask Lady Margaret what she meant. It was here that the young Katharine and Arthur spent the Christmas after they were married. It is a large black and white house built around dark oak timbers, with panelling and grand fireplaces.

I have only just arrived, but I love it already. If I close my eyes, I can imagine it all that time ago decorated in the prickly green and bright red of holly with candles making it all cosy and Christmassy. I hope we shall have a good Yuletide here too. It may be a while before I have my own court again and I intend to make the most of it. Maybe I might even shake off that recurring dream about the river that runs with blood, if I feel at peace here.

The Shakespeare family visited, and Abigail says the play is coming along well. That will certainly help make the entertainments go with a bang and I am looking forward to seeing how everyone reacts to it. Little John is crawling now and getting into all sorts of mischief. Like his father, he must be watched constantly.

3rd October

Like me, Marion doesn't like moving around.

"It makes me feel seasick, Madam. Especially when my heart, if I have one, is tied to Ludlow. I have stayed there so many centuries. This travelling is making me giddy."

"I know what you mean, Marion."

I answered her this morning after the fire was lit but before my ladies came to dress me, which was our usual time to talk.

"I only spent nine years in London before we got ripped away from it, but I still feel it in my bones every day, calling me back."

"Yes, feeling called back, yes. As though by some stretching, invisible thread. That is how it feels. But imagine hundreds of years, Princess."

I didn't know what to say. Homesickness is a terrible thing. I tried to reassure her.

"Once the play is done, Marion, I will see your stone carried carefully back to Ludlow. I am not sure they will let me go back there now. My father seems to have other ideas in store for my future. I promise I won't forget to do this though. And you will have my undying gratitude."

"I'd give you mine, Your Highness. But I'm dead already!"

We laughed, which brought my ladies to the door, and Marion faded quickly, a little sparkle of frost in the air the only indication I'd had spectral company.

"Who were you laughing with, Your Highness?" asked Cecily.

I just smiled.

25th November

I went to visit the players today, since they were in Worcester. They were performing a rather dull pageant about some saint or other I'd never heard of. When it was over, I gave them Mistress Shakespeare's script. Now it was finished, and I had approved it, they would need to learn their lines. I cautioned them to keep everything about it secret and guard their pages with their lives. That made them take notice.

"Now, Mister Shakespeare, in this play, you will take the part of the King. You are larger than life. It will suit you."

"But the King is not the best part Your Highness, nor the largest," he said, flicking through the work. "I always take the largest part!"

"Aye, you take the largest part of the pheasant too!" shouted one of his companion players, a short, tubby man with a smattering of red beard.

The company laughed. Mister Shakespeare grinned, but I could see he was a little put out.

"You shall do as you are told, Mister Shakespeare, and be glad I have singled you out as fit to play a monarch!"

He bowed and grunted. I ought to punish him for insolence, but I like him too much.

"Who shall play the lady ghost, Your Highness?" asked one of the taller teenagers, who was there to play the female parts, owing to still having a high voice and no whiskers on his chin.

"That part is taken care of," I said, smiling. "You will see who plays her on the night, and not before."

1st December

Hazel and I were so preoccupied changing clothes, my double doing an impression of Professor Duwes exploding into angry French as she did, that we did not notice a knock on the privy chamber door, nor Lizzie Pole coming quietly in. She gasped.

"What, what are you doing?" she asked, seeing us both in a state of mid-princess.

"Lizzie! Lizzie, come, sit."

I guided her to the wooden chair by the bed. She looked as though she might faint, being paler than usual.

"Do not be distressed, Lizzie," said Hazel, also worried by the look of her fellow servant.

"You were, you are... swapping clothes? Changing places?"

Hazel and I looked at one another. There seemed little point in denying it. There wasn't really any other explanation. Even Lizzie wasn't dim enough to think we were just dressing up.

"Can you keep a secret, Lizzie?" asked Hazel.

"Even from your mother and grandmother?" I asked. "For your princess?"

She thought for a minute, then nodded.

"I...I... think so. If it is very important."

"Oh, it is."

We explained what we'd been doing. Of course, we

made it sound much grander than just getting me out of lessons. It was a scheme to fall back on in case my life was in danger.

"I see," she said quietly.

"In fact, Lizzie, you might do us a very great favour by being brought into our plans."

"Might I?"

"Oh yes," I continued. "For not another soul knows about this. If something were to happen to either of us, if Hazel got into difficulties pretending to me be, or if I were hauled off to the tower for doing something wrong as a servant, then it would be you we would rely on to make sure all was set right."

"Me? What could I do?"

"You would have to come running to find the other of us and quickly. Could you do that?" I asked.

She nodded.

"And for such a great service to your future queen, you would of course be well rewarded."

"I would?"

"Yes indeed. But can you keep the secret, Lizzie, that's the thing. No-one must know. Otherwise, England's enemies might find out."

"Oh! I shall not tell a soul Your Highness. Not a soul. That, that *is* you, isn't it, Your Highness?"

I laughed: "Yes, it is me. If you are ever in doubt, you can ask us to speak French."

"Ha!" Hazel laughed. "That's not fair. True, but not fair!"

"Or I can point to the mole on your neck, Your Highness," Lizzie mumbled timidly.

And so now, we had an accomplice, one with more sense

than I had granted her. But it had shaken us both a little, being found out. We decided to leave our role-swapping for a while, not least in case there was a day it was really needed. Besides, it was not long until Christmas, and there would be fewer lessons and court petitions now, and a great deal more parties.

24th December

Christmas Eve came along quickly and so began a dull day, with the prospect of some of the last petitions at court before the festivities. I was not feeling well, having a slight headache. What I really needed was some fresh air, not to be cooped up with the public and their troubles, being advised or goaded by various lords. I decided to let Hazel take the brunt of it. We had not taken on our disguises for quite some time after all. Not since the day Lizzie had discovered us. As the fog outside cleared a little and some rays of sunshine managed to hit the window, my mind was made up. And what an important choice it turned out to be! If I had stayed and performed my duty, I might very well be dead!

I summoned Hazel via the chamber maid and gave her the signal we used, offering her some water from my ewer. We swapped places before the other ladies came to dress me, as usual. I went to the stables and told Matthew I had her Highness' permission to take Sheba out for some exercise. He always checked that I had the letter I gave her on such occasions. A loyal and careful servant is Matthew.

We were gently trotting back from the small copse when I saw Lizzie Pole dashing towards us, her skirts flying with one hand desperately holding her cap to her head. We trotted to her, but she could not speak for want of breath.

"What, Lizzie? What is it?"

"Oh Madam!" was all she could manage between great gulps of air. The waiting was awful. Eventually she spluttered: "Hazel. Poison!" and pointed at the house.

I pulled her up onto Sheba's back behind me and set off.

"Ride like the wind, madam, do!" Lizzie yelled.

We managed a light breeze, Sheba's little legs doing their best. We rode hard back to the manor and whipped around into the stables faster than we had ever done before. I threw myself down and Matthew helped Lizzie dismount.

"Where is she? What happened? Lizzie?"

The poor girl looked dazed and was still exhausted from her run.

"They took her to bed, Your Highness."

"Highness?" said Matthew, confused.

I grabbed Lizzie's hand and we ran as fast as we could. I had to leave her at the bottom of the staircase, for she was out of breath again so quickly, and no wonder. I burst into my own chambers, and threw off Hazel's cap.

"How does she?" I shouted, in my own voice, trusting the authority I bore to come through. But our disguises had fooled everyone.

"Very ill, Hazel, very ill," said Lady Catherine quietly, trying to ease me back the way I came, away from the pale figure in my bed. I saw Lady Margaret right by her, listening to Hazel's whispers.

"No, no, we will not leave you. What a notion!" said Margaret.

The deception would have to end.

"Everyone but Lady Margaret must leave the room." I

said commandingly. "This poison, I know it, it is contagious."

This was enough for everyone but the aforesaid Margaret, and Lady Catherine, who stayed resolutely.

"Ladies, I said, shutting the door firmly behind Lizzie, who had just made it to the top of the stairs, "I am Mary, not Hazel. We swapped clothes as a jape this morning. What has happened? Tell me exactly and precisely."

"What are you talking about?" asked Margaret, beyond confused.

"It's true," said Lizzie. "This is the Princess. Look, she has a mole here, on her neck, and Hazel does not."

Lady Margaret looked at the patient's neck, then at mine, before spluttering: "This *is* Mary. But what is going on, why the deception? Did you know this would happen?"

"No, of course not, it was just for fun. Not so now. Tell me what has happened and help me become Mary again."

They did just that. I changed into some fresh clothes, and they told me what they knew.

Hazel had gone into the Great Hall and begun hearing petitions. But before the first was even done, she put her hand to her forehead and complained of a severe headache. Then a rash appeared on her face and neck, and she fell forward. It was only Dudley catching her that stopped her collapsing entirely. They carried her to bed and called the apothecary.

"He said it looked like poisoning and that we must prepare for the worst, Mary! And all the while we were thinking it was you!" Margaret burst into tears.

My head was clear, I had to save Hazel. But there was also a great advantage presenting itself to me over my enemies, who must even now be thinking that they have successfully killed the heir to the throne.

"Did the apothecary say what kind of poison he suspected? Or how violent it might be?"

"He said the rash made him suspect belladonna. But Hazel is a country girl, she would know not to touch that!" Lady Catherine explained.

"Indeed, as would I!" I looked around the room, deep in thought. "And what has she had to eat? Was it tested first?"

"Everything was tested by Constance and Cecily. They are both quite well, if a little hysterical."

"Understandable."

At this point Hazel reached out her hand, obviously in pain. She was trying to get a cup of water. Lady Margaret began to pour it.

"Wait!" I shouted, grabbing the ewer from her.

She put the cup down. Floating in the jug of water, instead of the sprig of mint I have been used to, was a similar-shaped but very different plant. A cutting of belladonna, with a few loose leaves bobbing in the water. My head swam. I had offered Hazel a glass of this water that very morning and declined one myself in my haste to ride.

"Get a fresh cup and fresh water, do it yourself, Lady Catherine," I ordered.

She ran to the kitchens whilst I racked my brain. Had I seen who placed the ewer today? And then the memory came into view. I knew who had done it.

"Put the ewer back down, Lady Margaret. We need it to identify the culprit, but then it must be smashed. Lizzie, have Clara fetched here along with two of the other girls please. It doesn't matter which." She curtsied and ran to her mission. Now I was alone with Lady Margaret and Hazel.

"Hazel, sweet girl, hold on. Lady Margaret, I think we must try the cure we know of before the apothecary returns. You know of what I speak."

She nodded: "But, Your Highness, we do not know the dose," her voice closed to a whisper. "We might kill her."

"If we don't, she will die anyway. It is called deadly for a reason."

She sighed and nodded.

It wasn't much of a plan, but it was all we had. She fetched the jar we had hidden in my monk's chest, and we carefully placed one tiny bean on a handkerchief. I had her keep her gloves on. She grated a tiny piece of the bean, barely a speck, into the palm of her hand. I nodded.

When Lady Catherine came back with the water, I placed the speck on Hazel's tongue and bid her swallow it. As Hazel sat up and drank the new poison down to kill the old one, Lizzie returned with Clara, Cecily and Anne.

The three young ladies looked confused. Here was the Princess, up, dressed and seemingly well, and someone else, wasn't it Hazel, lying in the royal bed? Clara, of all, looked most distressed and alarmed.

"Clara, won't you bring me that ewer there, I am so thirsty," I commanded.

The girl picked it up, but her hands were shaking. She brought it over to me.

"Don't you want a glass, Your Highness?"

"Oh no, I am that parched I shall drink straight from the jug. But you look hot yourself from running up the stairs, Clara. Would you take some water?"

She looked at the jug, with the deadly leaves still in the

water, looked at me, and knew the game was up. She shrieked, and dropped the ewer, smashing it to bits.

"Oh, I'm so clumsy!" she said, fooling no-one.

"You are not clumsy, you are a poisoner!" I screamed – releasing my rage.

The two guards stationed outside the door came running in.

"Take her and lock her away," I said. "She has tried to murder me!"

The guards grabbed an arm each and marched her away, her screams of protest gradually fading.

"You are all witnesses," I said to the ladies, pointing to the deadly leaves and stem on the floor amongst the shards of glass.

"She's getting worse! Oh Mary, she's getting worse!"

Lady Margaret's cries brought me back to the real problem. Hazel was coming out in a great sweat, and her forehead was dripping. She was clutching her stomach in pain.

"Best get a pot," I said sensibly, but Lizzie was already there with one.

"It might mean the cure is working, Lady Margaret. Let us not panic yet. She may well recover. Pray, ladies, pray!"

The dear souls gathered around Hazel's bedside and prayed their rosaries. I too had my head bowed, but rather than pray for Hazel's life I was praying for revenge. Clara was merely a pawn in a deadly game. She will go to the tower, but I am determined she shall not go alone.

25th December

The court was in uproar this Christmas morning, rumours of my impending death running rife, as I wanted it so. I had Clara's imprisonment kept secret, and slept in Lady Catherine's room, whilst Lady Margaret stayed at Hazel's bedside, with orders to report any changes to me.

At the rise of the sun, I went to Hazel. The apothecary had come back and been shown the contents of the ewer. He came prepared with his leeches and stayed the night in the next room. Today he reported no great decline, but no great recovery either. Hazel was weak and pale. She had stopped sweating so much though, was no longer vomiting and the rash had faded. I remain hopeful.

"If the poison was going to kill her, surely it would have done so by now?" I pronounced rather than asked.

He looked grave, and his voice held all the condescension a trained medic could hold for a mere girl, albeit a royal one. "It is sometimes slow-working, Your Highness. It depends how much water she had."

I made no comment, just squeezed Hazel's hand and prayed to God that she might somehow hold on.

I had important business with Abigail Shakespeare this morning. She was already staying with her husband and young John in the guest apartments, much to the disapproval of my steward and chancellor. They think of me as a mere child no doubt. But I am the Princess, and maybe, by now, I have some idea of what I am doing.

"We need to change the script," I said to Mistress Shakespeare and her husband, as they were getting ready for church.

"Change it? Now? But the play is staged tomorrow night!" she said, with understandable alarm.

"Are you quite well?" asked Richard, bouncing John up and down in his arms. "We heard you were taken very bad…"

"I am quite well, thank you," I said. "And in order to catch the men who just tried to have me killed, we need to change the play."

"Tried to have you killed? Your Highness!" Abigail shrieked.

"They failed, obviously. But one of my ladies is very poorly as a result and I'd appreciate your prayers for her…and your secrecy."

"Yes of course!" said Richard, as his wife nodded earnestly. "And don't worry about the play. If anyone can do it – it's my Abigail."

"I will not be at chapel. I want my enemies to imagine they are near success. But tell your company, Mister Shakespeare, not to be alarmed if I do a little acting myself.

26th December

Hazel was showing more improvement this morning and I began to believe she would recover. A great relief. But the fright it has given us, and the audacity of Clara and those backing her, has made me angrier than I knew I could be.

I dressed myself as dear Hazel, for I wanted people to remain concerned about Princess Mary's illness, spreading my own rumours and half-truths today to feed the lie. I did not mention poison, but I did speak of evil acts and wicked wrongs. In the Great Hall, I saw Gravenor coming to speak to the players, so I ducked behind the curtain of the stage.

"I'm not sure that the entertainments should continue, Mister Shakespeare," Gravenor said, interrupting rehearsals. "It does not seem right under the circumstances."

"What circumstances would they be, then?" asked Richard, all feigned innocence.

"Haven't you heard, man? The Princess is gravely ill. Maybe even at death's door!"

"God's Truth? Where did you hear that?"

"But it is the talk of the castle, Mister Shakespeare! You cannot be so wrapped up in your acting that you did not notice Mary was not at church yesterday. On Christmas Day!"

"There might be lots of reasons for missing church, my Lord. I've missed it myself at Easter before with a hangover. And I think you'll find it's Princess Mary, or Her Highness to you."

I grinned as I listened.

"The ten-year-old Princess of Wales is unlikely to have a hangover," Gravenor continued. "From what I hear it is a deathly illness. A rash, they say, and such pains in the head as might kill her."

He did sound very knowledgeable and quite excited. I wanted to let my temper go and rip into him right away, but I knew it better to play the waiting game.

"Her Highness is adamant that we proceed, Lord Grovellor."

"Gravenor."

"Whatever. The Princess is very keen for the play to proceed. I know who I take my orders from, and it isn't you."

Mister Shakespeare came back behind the stage curtain then and grinned at me. He knew it was me straight away, used to seeing through the veneer of costumes.

I went back upstairs to check on Hazel. It felt strange to think that if anything had happened to me, she could have become the Princess maybe without anyone realising. But it was her, the poor soul, who had been poisoned. And it was all my fault. If I hadn't been so lazy and wanted to duck out of lessons and boring court sessions, this would not have happened. And yet... I now had high hopes she would recover, and the whole thing was just too delicious an opportunity to pass up. I could frighten the wits out of Gravenor and Puce far more than I'd thought. How it would shock them to see me looking quite well!

It was immense fun to hide once more behind the curtains in my servant's disguise this evening and watch the court fill the chairs in the Great Hall ready for the play. There was a lot of chatter and excitement. A princess's demise was certainly something worth gossiping about, for sure, but there were also those who were quietly wiping away tears.

"Well, Your Highness," whispered Richard Shakespeare, with his theatrical crown upon his head and his face changed by actor's paints, "here we are, me pretending to be royal and you pretending not to be. Ready to frighten some villains, eh?"

"I am very ready, Richard. I know my players won't let me down. Let the scheming commence!"

My empty throne at the far end of the hall looked most strange, and everyone kept looking at it until Dudley made an announcement: "Ladies and Gentlemen, Her Royal Highness the Princess of Wales is indisposed this evening."

A rush of voices began more conjecture. Dudley held up his hand to be allowed to finish. "That is all I am at liberty to say. However, she has given the command that the festivities should continue unabated. She is particularly keen for everyone to see the play commissioned for tonight. Please enjoy, *The Lady's Revenge!*"

He bowed and the minstrels up in the gallery played a fanfare as the curtains opened.

The first act of the play was about two lords in the court of a king who were both foolish and wicked. One was very tall and thin with pale hair and a streak of red in his moustache, the other was short and plump and kept slopping food and drink down himself. The audience were quick to realise who was being mocked, and so were Gravenor and Puce. Everyone was laughing at them, and they had to sit there and take it. I had been worried that they might try to storm out and so posted guards on the doors. I almost wanted them to, as that would make them look sillier still.

There was much tomfoolery and slapstick, with Mister Shakespeare as the king in his court, making mincemeat out of the two noblemen and showing them up at every opportunity. The audience were crying with laughter and whooping with joy. The Master of the Revels was making his talents felt. Beer was brought around and plenty of it. The looser tongues were tonight, the better, for I wanted people off their guard.

The second half, which Abigail, who was keeping to her room with the baby tonight, had rewritten, was very different, and quickly took a darker turn. The wicked lords schemed to get their own favourite on the throne by wanting the King's sweet and good daughter dead. They consulted witches with poisonous brews and magicians with hexes and all manner of evil plans were concocted. The audience booed, jeered and even hissed. Their favourite was an illegitimate nephew of the King, whom I had insisted was called Stephen, for Marion's sake. Her stone was propped up against the stage throne, as part of the scenery. Tonight was her revenge too.

In the end, the wicked lords conned a young servant girl into putting belladonna into the good princess's water jug. What Gravenor and Puce had failed to notice, as they watched the truth unveiled on stage, was two guards bringing Clara in to watch at the very back of the hall.

The princess took one sip and fell into extremely over-dramatic death throes. The room went deathly quiet and cold as the pretend princess lay dead. Icicles started to form on the platters, candles began to smoke, and glasses and tankards began to frost over. Marion entered, stage left, more visible than usual, in a special effort, and her silvery form raced around the room before settling in the centre of the stage.

"You have killed me, foolish child!" she said, in icy tones.

The whole room gaped in horror and wonder, unsure if they were seeing a real phantom, or some ingenious new trick by Mister Shakespeare and his troupe. Some of them (including the men) screamed, and two servant girls ran shrieking to the kitchens. Marion looked entirely splendid, all shimmering white. The spell remained in place until the young lad playing the serving girl cried out in agonizing sorrows, all a tremble: "Oh! What have I done, what have I done? Dear sweet, innocent lady, who might have been Queen!"

And then he fainted, which hadn't been in the script. As I had planned, it was all too much for the guilty parties. Clara screamed: "That's just how it was, just how it was. They made me do it!"

I took that as my cue. I had changed into my royal robes and came out from behind the curtain to gasps and cheers, as Marion curtsied and gradually faded to nothing. The room warmed to my presence.

"Who made you do what, Clara?" I asked coolly. "What are you saying?"

"Them! Those Lords there – Puce and Gravenor! They told me to put poison in your water!"

There was a great intake of shocked breath that reverberated around the huge room.

"I've never seen that girl before in my life!" said Puce, quickly. "I don't know what she's talking about."

"She's your niece, isn't she?" said one of the servants.

How delicious, I thought. That would explain the puffy face, too.

"Well, I've certainly never seen her before," said Gravenor, his face growing ever paler.

"Rubbish!" called someone else. "I've seen her working in your kitchens!"

Others joined in, adding their testimonies as Clara nodded and cried. I walked to the throne and raised my hand to ask for hush. It felt good to be back.

"And, Clara, these gentlemen had you place belladonna in my drinking water?"

She nodded.

"I can't hear you?"

"Yes," she sobbed. "Yes. I am so sorry."

"You are sorry you got caught, I am sure. What is truly

awful for you is that it was not I who was poisoned, but one of my dear ladies, who has been lying at death's door for several days."

The court was angry and sad and were calling for justice. They smelled blood like a pack of hounds and rounded on Puce and Gravenor, grabbing them by the arms and hauling them up before the throne.

"They meant for me to die so they could put that upstart Richmond on the throne of England!" I called out, hoping that this would be remembered. There was booing. "God has sought to spare me, and my loyal servant."

"To the tower with them, to the tower!" one cried, others echoing his demands.

Lord Dudley came forward, keen to calm things down. I nodded to him.

"Yes, to the Tower they must surely go. See to it, Dudley. Have them confess. And when they do, mark that they tell from whom they received the order to poison me."

I looked straight at Gravenor, still pale and shaken after seeing not one, but seemingly two ghosts before him. My heart did a little jig of triumph as he looked away. He will die a most painful death before the spring is out, I wager.

The guards took them all away. I ordered more beer – for it was still Christmastide. I stole one look at Clara as she too was marched out the door. She looked small and tired, her eyes pleading with me. But whatever hold these two had over her, she was still a poisoner, and must be punished. It was over. I had won.

1527

4th February

It will be strange to leave the Marches after all this time. It was here that I discovered my father's dreadful deeds and learned how to thwart murderers. I have saved my own skin and my own soul, I believe, with the help of Hazel and Marion, from both of whom I must now take my leave.

Hazel is yet too weak to be moved, but I have given instructions for her to have the best care, and from one of my own apothecaries who is far better to be trusted than the old poison merchant. She will recover, I am told, and when she does, I shall have her return to her family, along with my eternal gratitude. If she continues to look like me as we age, I may have use of her again one day.

5th February

Marion was still weak after her own fantastic exertions in the play. She has only managed to appear to me a couple of mornings this year, and I could barely see her form. It was only the chill in the room today that alerted me to her presence, as I woke from the now familiar nightmare of the bloody hunt in the river.

"Marion, you have been a good friend and I will not forget your service to me, and to the realm." I said, hoping she could hear me.

"Thank you, young madam, dear Highness," she said softly, and curtsied to me.

"We leave here tomorrow. I am having the stone carried carefully back to the castle," I said. "I hope that you will find your strength returns there, and that perhaps your soul will feel more at ease."

I sensed, rather than saw her smile of relief.

"I am glad. I shall be more myself at home. Thank you. I hope to see you again."

And with that, she was gone. The fire flickered back into flame, and I wondered if that was the last time we'd meet. For the rest of my life, I would be glad to hear tales of the White Lady of Ludlow Castle.

15th February

The journey back to London seemed to take such a short time. When we neared the capital I asked Dudley if I might visit our friends in the Tower. He seemed a little dubious at first.

"They have been there some weeks, Your Highness. They are not…They are not as they were. You may find them a little altered."

This made me a little excited, which is doubtless wicked, but they did try to murder me. I think I am entitled to be glad of their suffering. Some Bible verse or other about mercy popped into my head but I waved it away. A future queen cannot be merciful unless it suits her. My grin surprised Dudley I think, but all he did was raise that left eyebrow (as he so often did) and say he would add the visit to the next day's itinerary.

16th February

There were a lot of stairs to climb. I have not been to the Tower before and had not realised how many rooms and cells were tucked away in the sprawling square of the building and its turrets. Lady Catherine accompanied me along with Dudley. Lady Margaret said she did not have the stomach for it, and no wonder, for I think her father was executed here.

We meant to see Clara first, but the guard informed us she was no longer here.

"That young lady has already been dispatched by the headsman," he said without any emotion at all. "She was only a commoner and mounted no defense."

I was sorry not to see her quivering here.

"Did she make any confessions?" I asked.

"Oh, a great many, Your Highness, though no two made any sense taken together. She was tired of the rack and would have told us anything. We had her sign some, but being only fifteen, they won't hold much weight."

I nodded my understanding. I tried to imagine the servant girl on the rack, but it gave me no comfort. I felt it ought to, after what she had done to Hazel, and meant to do to me.

Puce was next. He and Gravenor were to be beheaded the following day. I wasn't sure yet if I wanted to see that. Lady Catherine said she thought it would not be a good idea. As we entered the cell, I didn't recognize my enemy at first. He had lost a lot of weight.

"Prison portions are a little lighter than you are used to, I imagine."

Puce said nothing.

"He won't speak, Your Highness," said the guard who was guiding us. "Couldn't shut him up at first. He confessed to everything. Even said he killed the Princes in the Tower."

The man laughed, a strange, unearthly sound in such grim surroundings. I wondered how he got through the day.

"Now he doesn't say a word. Dead already. Some of them do that."

He walked over to Puce, who was sat motionless and jabbed him with the tip of his boot.

"Never mind. All over tomorrow," said the guard.

Lord Gravenor we went to last. The change in him was the most shocking. Away from the comfort and security of position and court, thrown into a dark and foul prison, he had lost all his cocksure manner and confidence. He saw me and fell on his knees, begging for his life to be spared. I noted with fascination that he had lost some fingers. The guard pulled him away and gave him a hefty whack across his cheekbone. He fell down.

"Mostly gibberish, now, this one," said the guard, who seemed rather cheerful. "I'll give him his due though, he lasted a while and said he acted alone. Not many do that."

I felt a grudging admiration for the once handsome man cradling himself on the straw next to me. Lady Catherine put her kerchief to her nose to keep the smell out. There were patches of blood on the floor, some fresher than others.

As we climbed back into the carriage, I was shaking a little. Dudley and Lady Catherine looked at me with some concern.

"Ruling is a very difficult thing," said Dudley. "Hard decisions have to be made. To show mercy would be so show weakness."

I nodded. They exchanged glances.

"These are people who wanted you dead, Princess Mary. They deserve this."

I nodded again but said nothing. I was thinking and trying not to feel too much. If God had made me to be Queen, to protect his church, there would be times again for killing, for prisons, for blood.

"I suppose they shall see a priest?" I asked when we were back in the coach.

"You are very good, Your Highness, to think of it. Yes, I believe all prisoners are granted that mercy," said Lady Catherine.

I can confess here in my diary, that I was hoping they wouldn't. I don't want to be in heaven with their kind. I know exactly where they ought to be sent, somewhere hot and fiery. That's where they belong.

At Hampton, I headed first for the mews, and joyfully greeted Guinevere. A younger falconer helped me take her for a flight. Hedges appeared at some point out of the dusk.

"You've not lost the knack, Miss," the old man said. "Truth be told, I think you have learned a thing or two whilst you were away."

"I rather think I have, Hedges," I said.

The goshawk flew delightedly round and round, before returning to the lure.

"I have worked out how to stay in the calm at the very centre and let the birds of prey circle around me until they are dizzy. I can lure and tame. I am no longer afraid of queening."

The falconer said nothing, just nodded and lit his pipe. I stroked Guinevere's head as she sat on my arm and smiled. Let them all parade around tomorrow and think I am their puppet. In two days' time I turn eleven. I shall show everyone how strong my heart and wings beat. I placed the hood back on the bird's head. They will not tame this princess so easily.

Also in this series...

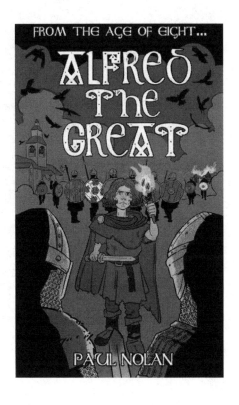

FROM THE AGE OF EIGHT...

ALFRED THE GREAT

PAUL NOLAN

ISBN: 9781914426025   UK £7.99

It's not easy being Anglo-Saxon royalty. As well as rampaging axe-happy Vikings, you're going to have your hands full fighting off rival members of your own family. Find out how Alfred became the last noble standing in this gripping royal read.

Also in this series...

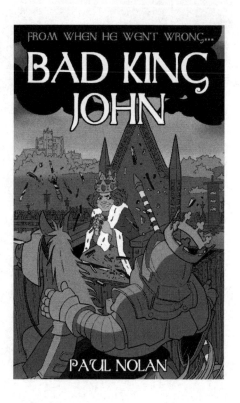

FROM WHEN HE WENT WRONG...

BAD KING JOHN

PAUL NOLAN

ISBN: 9781906132521   UK £7.99

Dishonest, cunning and cruel, King John was so bad that even his mother despised him! Fighting his own brothers for the crown, he stabbed them in the back at every opportunity. Meet the prince who put the evil into medieval in this ripping royal read.